"Tell Me How I Was Hurt. Who Shot Me?"

"I don't know. I wish I did. You disappeared. You were there...and then suddenly you were gone." Her voice shook and she dropped her chin.

The frustration welled up, making him blind with need. He grabbed her shoulders and lasered a kiss across her lips....

When at last he had to take a breath, he broke away from her with a jolt, gasping for air. Gazing at her kiss-swollen lips, he knew he still didn't remember, still was at a loss for a past life.

The fact that she knew more about him than he knew about himself was nearly unbearable. The woman in his arms had a history, and she held the key to his past, as well.

Dear Reader,

Summer vacation is simply a state of mind...so create your dream getaway by reading six new love stories from Silhouette Desire!

Begin your romantic holiday with *A Cowboy's Pursuit* by Anne McAllister. This MAN OF THE MONTH title is the author's 50th book and part of her CODE OF THE WEST miniseries. Then learn how a Connelly bachelor mixes business with pleasure in *And the Winner Gets...Married!* by Metsy Hingle, the sixth installment of our exciting DYNASTIES: THE CONNELLYS continuity series.

An unlikely couple swaps insults and passion in Maureen Child's *The Marine & the Debutante*—the latest of her popular BACHELOR BATTALION books. And a night of passion ignites old flames in *The Bachelor Takes a Wife* by Jackie Merritt, the final offering in TEXAS CATTLEMAN'S CLUB: THE LAST BACHELOR continuity series.

In *Single Father Seeks...* by Amy J. Fetzer, a businessman and his baby captivate a CIA agent working under cover as their nanny. And in Linda Conrad's *The Cowboy's Baby Surprise,* an amnesiac FBI agent finds an undreamed-of happily-ever-after when he's reunited with his former partner and lover.

Read these passionate, powerful and provocative new Silhouette Desire romances and enjoy a sensuous summer vacation!

Joan Marlow Golan

Joan Marlow Golan
Senior Editor, Silhouette Desire

Please address questions and book requests to:
Silhouette Reader Service
U.S.: 3010 Walden Ave., P.O. Box 1325, Buffalo, NY 14269
Canadian: P.O. Box 609, Fort Erie, Ont. L2A 5X3

The Cowboy's Baby Surprise
LINDA CONRAD

Hope you enjoy
the book!

Linda Conrad

Silhouette®
Desire®

Published by Silhouette Books
America's Publisher of Contemporary Romance

SILHOUETTE BOOKS

ISBN 0-373-76446-4

THE COWBOY'S BABY SURPRISE

LINDA CONRAD

was born in Brazil to a commercial pilot dad and a mother whose first gift was a passion for stories. She was raised in South Florida and has been a dreamer and a storyteller for as long as she can remember. Linda claims her earliest memories are of sitting in her mother's lap, listening to a beloved storybook or searching through the picture books in the library to find that special one.

When Linda met and married her own dream-come-true hero, he fostered another of her other inherited vices— being a vagabond. They moved to seven different states in seven years, finally becoming enchanted with and settling down in the Rio Grande Valley of Texas.

Reality anchored Linda to their Texas home long enough to raise a daughter and become a stockbroker and certified financial planner. Her whole world suddenly changed when her widowed mother suffered a disabling stroke and Linda spent a year as her caretaker. Before her mother's second and fatal stroke, she begged Linda to go back to her dreams —to finally tell the stories buried within her heart.

Linda's hobbies are reading, growing roses and experiencing new things. However, her real passion is "passion"—reading about it, writing about it and living it. She believes that true passion and intensity for life and love are seductive—they consume the soul and make life's trials and tribulations worth all the effort.

"I am extremely grateful that today I can live my dreams by being able to share the passionate stories and lovable characters that have lived deep within me for so long," Linda declares.

For Emily Olmstead, Sarah Gross and Donna Kordela, the greatest critique group ever. This book never would have happened without your valuable input.

And to my sister, Susan Zyne, and to my dearest husband, J.C. Both of you believed in me always, and that made all the difference in the world.

One

"**Y**ou want me to take my baby on a stakeout?" Carley Mills shoved her chair back from the desk and stood to confront her boss. "Have you totally lost your mind?" she muttered in her typical lazy, Southern accent.

"This isn't a 'stakeout,' for crying out loud. Will you listen to the proposition before you go jumping to conclusions?" Carley's boss, Reid Sorrels, towered over her, and she felt the brunt of his notoriously dark stare.

As the busy assistant field operations manager for the Houston office of the FBI and agent in charge of Operation Rock-a-Bye, Reid got to the point. "Besides, you know I'd never do anything to put my goddaughter in jeopardy, don't you?" He plopped down in one of the two secretary chairs facing Carley's desk.

She stiffened her spine to face him and thought of how far she'd come in the last eighteen months. She'd been so devastated when her partner and lover, Witt Davidson, disappeared that she couldn't have confronted a flea, let alone someone as burly and determined as her boss.

Witt had vanished into thin air. She'd always thought she was a strong person, able to cope with anything life threw her way. She prided herself on being able to help others with their problems and emotional traumas. But the stress of not knowing what happened to the man who fathered her child had nearly broken her.

All right, so he'd never said he loved her. And he certainly hadn't shown any enthusiasm for settling down with a family...but Witt hadn't really known he had a family, either. Carley hadn't given him a chance to know. She'd been so desperate to be sure he really cared for her that she'd put off telling him until they could get away from their jobs and truly be alone.

But right in the middle of a major sting operation at Lake Houston one fateful August night Witt disappeared. One minute he'd been smiling at her and heading off to check out a suspicious-looking truck— then he was gone. Without a trace.

They'd been so close to a tentative commitment. She'd known he was skittish about settling down, but she was positive she could have made him admit his love. Despite her conviction that Witt was a good man and wouldn't run away, the doubts continually plagued her.

"You still with me, Carl?" Reid broke into her

thoughts, and she set her jaw to tackle her immediate problem.

Carley edged around the beat-up oak desk until she stood a couple of feet from her boss, a man whose chronological age placed him at about thirty-three, only a few years older than she. Regardless of chronological age, he was light years ahead in wisdom and strength.

She leaned her rear against the desktop and forced a smile at the man who'd been her savior more times than she could count. "Of course I know you wouldn't hurt Cami...intentionally. But to uproot her and go chasing off to some remote part of the West sounds like it might not be in her best interest, either."

Reid scowled. "You still haven't listened. That part of the Texas-Mexico border is perfectly civilized." He ran a few fingers through his chestnut-colored hair, disturbing the lines of a new, trim cut. "The youth ranch is only thirty miles outside McAllen, Texas. It's a city of over a hundred thousand people, and less than a day's drive from here."

"Fine. Great. But what earthly good would I be at a ranch? I've never set foot on one in my life."

"Damn it, Carley, I asked you to keep an open mind and listen. The place is essentially an institution, an orphanage...although they don't call them that these days. You're trained in child psychology...and they need a child psychologist. You'll hardly even know you're on a ranch."

With a huge sigh, Carley braced herself for whatever came next. She had a feeling another drastic life change was headed her way. Since a few months before Cami's birth, the Bureau had refused to use her for undercover work. Lately she'd spent most of her time certifying the paperwork for the Mexican babies that the operation had recovered, and verifying the children to be fit for the return to their native country.

Now, all of sudden, the FBI needed her to do surveillance at the border? And to take Cami with her? The whole thing sounded ridiculous.

"The foster home is run by the Texas church council, but these kinds of places never have enough money to operate." Reid gave her a few more details. The way he scrutinized her face with his deep-set eyes let Carley know he was closely judging her reactions. "There are always more children than the funds to keep them. The church runs both a cattle ranch and a citrus farm to help provide the means to keep the children's home afloat."

"But what exactly do you expect me to do there?"

"I expect you to do what you're best at...work with the children. All the kids there are throwaways. The babies have been dumped and are unadoptable until the state determines parental rights. The older children are either youthful offenders sent there for rehabilitation or they're disabled in some way. As you can imagine, all of them have emotional problems."

Yep, he knew her well. Her imagination ran rampant with thoughts of the cast-off children who needed the care only she could give them. "But what will I be doing for Operation Rock-a-Bye?"

"The border is where the action is right now." Reid smiled at her with only the corners of his eyes. "You know we've tracked some of the scum from this international baby-selling ring to the McAllen area. Just pay attention to what's going on."

He shifted in his too-small seat and looked decidedly uncomfortable. "We have an agent in the area, Manny Sanchez, who's undercover as a veterinarian's assistant. The job enables him to travel along the Rio Grande talking to farm and ranch laborers. With his information we've stopped dozens of *coyotes* in the act of bringing Mexican babies across the border."

Reid sat forward in his chair and put his elbows on his knees. "Manny heard a rumor, spreading through the illegal population a while back, that a few of the babies showing up at the church home are coming from across the river, not from the usual state agencies."

He stood to drive home his point. "Manny's been working every day with the vet on the church's cattle, doing the yearly inseminations and inoculations, but we need someone inside the place. Someone with access to the children...and to the records."

Carley knew she was sunk. "And how am I going to get the job?"

"The job is yours. One of the elders on the church-council is an old friend of mine. The person who used to hold the position had a sudden 'family emergency.' The home administrator is expecting you and Cami. He doesn't know your real identity...just that you're a psychologist and a single mother in need of work. His church council supervisor has vouched for you."

"Swell. And when..." Something in her boss's eyes stopped her cold.

"There's something else. Something urgent."

Ah. Here comes the real reason. Carley held her breath and waited.

Reid turned his back and paced to the far corner of the tiny, cluttered office. "Manny Sanchez worked with your old partner, Witt, on an undercover operation near El Paso about five years ago. The mission lasted only a short time, and the two men saw each other for mere minutes, but…''

Carley's heart paused in midbeat. ''This is about Witt? Has there been a break in the investigation into his disappearance?'' She flew at Reid's wide back and, catching him off guard, spun him to face her. ''Tell me what this is about.''

''Take it easy.'' Reid cleared his throat, straightened his back and resumed his agent-in-charge demeanor. ''Special Agent Charleston Mills, you know the Bureau will never give up until we uncover what happened to Davidson. Every FBI agent in the world keeps one eye open for him at all times. We don't just *lose* agents.''

Reid gently pulled Carley's hands from his shoulders and held on to her wrists, making her listen carefully to his explanation. ''Manny believed a fellow working on the ranch bares an uncanny resemblance to Davidson.''

Carley's mouth dropped open, and the room started to spin. ''But…but…''

Reid threw an arm around her shoulder and guided her into a chair. ''You need some water?''

She shook her head but still couldn't manage to speak.

''We've verified it's Davidson from his prints. But…he isn't using his own name and didn't recognize Manny.''

Carley found her voice. ''Why didn't you bring him home? Is he being held against his will? Is it possible that's why he couldn't admit who he is?''

Reid shrugged. ''Not likely. In the first place, can

you picture someone holding Davidson against his will for eighteen months?''

A smile threatened to break out on her face, but she held back, only managing to shake her head once more. So many questions ran through her mind that her own needs were pushed aside for the time being.

''No? Me, neither.'' Reid sat back on the desk the same as Carley had done earlier. ''In the second place, Manny says this fellow comes and goes whenever he wants...seems to have the run of the place.''

''Then what's going on? If it's Witt, why isn't he home?'' Carley felt her blood begin to boil. How could Witt stay away? How could he do such a thing to the agency? To her?

Reid stood to pace, then stopped, and Carley sensed he was forcing himself to face her again. ''We've done some checking with his co-workers and have come to a startling conclusion. Davidson's lost his memory and has no idea who he is.

''Amnesia seems like the only explanation that makes much sense. Before I drag him back here and institutionalize him, I figure you're the perfect person to try to help him regain his memory...you being a psychologist and in love with him and all.''

Carley was stunned speechless. Witt an amnesia victim? Strong, dangerous Witt Davidson needed her help?

''I can't spare you much time,'' Reid warned. ''But we're moving the bulk of our operation to the border in the general vicinity of the foster ranch. You go work on bringing Witt back to us, Carley. But keep in touch. If you need anything, let me know.''

Twenty-four hours later Carley introduced herself to Gabe Diaz, a man about sixty with gray-streaked hair and kindly eyes behind round, thick glasses. A former church preacher and currently the home administrator, Gabe welcomed her and showed her through the main house.

She'd spent six hours of the last day just driving to this godforsaken place. Carley had checked it out on the map and had the auto club trace the directions in yellow marker. Nevertheless, many times on the trip she'd been convinced she'd gotten lost. No one could live this far out of the way or survive with all this bleak landscape.

Perfectly civilized, my foot.

Carley spent most of the trying, six-hour drive daydreaming about the last time she'd seen Witt. About how his blond hair and boy-next-door good looks made him the perfect undercover agent. Criminals never suspected the steely danger lurking within him. But the man also had a tender side, as she knew only too well. Carley nearly drove herself and Cami off the road remembering his gentle caresses and his seductive kisses.

With Cami buckled securely in her car seat, they'd gone for several hours without so much as seeing a gas station. Every couple of hours Carley had pulled off the road to give Cami a drink or change her diaper. Finally the car had crested a small incline, and she'd been relieved to see the outskirts of a real city.

The city of McAllen, located on the Texas-Mexico border at a bend in the Rio Grande, was home to over a hundred thousand people. In every direction, Carley saw shopping, schools, churches. Everything looked new and clean and prosperous, as the city sprang out of the open range to the north. Unfortunately, the map to the foster home routed her the west, away from this sparkling little city, and into a dangerous looking and desolate countryside.

She'd followed the road along the Rio Grande until she'd finally found the turnoff to the children's home and ranch. Her car had bumped down a pitted, caliche roadway past what appeared to be miles of nothing but cactus and cows.

The end of the road had brought them to a handful of buildings and barns. She'd seen an imposing-looking two-story house surrounded by trees, dirt and a wide black-topped parking lot. The flapping wood sign on an old post had said, Casa de Valle. "House in the Valley," their temporary new home.

"I need to speak to one of the counselors," Preacher Gabe said, bringing her back to the present. "Look around for yourself after you settle Cami into the day room. The older children watch over the babies and toddlers there. They're real good with the babies. You'll be impressed."

Carley handed Cami off to a sweet-looking young girl and dumped their luggage in the upstairs room assigned to them. She didn't even bother to change clothes before heading outside. With no earthly idea of where to begin looking for a man on a ranch, she was determined to track down this person who was supposed to be Witt—that very afternoon.

At first Carley had been shocked by Reid's idea of amnesia. But she quickly adjusted and readied herself for any contingency before packing and making the long drive. Besides her personal gear and the various Bureau-issued weapons and equipment, she'd armed herself with information. She remembered a few things about amnesia from school, but if this was indeed Witt, and he was suffering from memory loss, she intended to help in any way she could.

She'd downloaded every scrap of information from the Internet and called on one of her former professors. What she'd found didn't give her much hope. Most amnesia victims either recovered their memories within a few weeks or, at most, a couple of months—or they never did. The thought of finding Witt after all this time, only to never really get him back, preyed on her mind.

"Maybe the shock of seeing you will jolt his memory," her professor had said. Oh please. If there is a God, it will be that simple.

The other standard piece of advice was not to force things—to let the memories return on their own. "Give him time. Losing your entire existence can be a very frightening proposition."

Easy for a distant professor to say, Carley thought. Much harder to accomplish when it was someone you loved who'd totally forgotten you.

When she stepped outside into the sun, not much appeared to be happening on this hot afternoon in the yard between the back door of the huge main house and the various outbuildings within walking distance. Carley wondered if everyone took a siesta after lunch in this part of the world.

"Excuse me, ma'am, you looking for something?" A cowboy in jeans, a plaid shirt and straw hat appeared out of the shadows and ambled toward her from one of the big, barn-like structures.

"Uh…yes. I'm looking for someone."

"And who would that be? You don't look like you'd be knowing anybody in these parts…if you don't mind me saying so, ma'am."

Carley looked down at herself. Still dressed in the wool-blend pants suit and short heels she'd worn for the trip, she guessed she probably didn't look much like she belonged in a barnyard. Now why hadn't she taken a minute to change into her jeans?

Before doing anything about that mistake, she needed to find a way out of her more immediate problem. Carley couldn't remember what name Reid had said Witt was using. Who the heck should she say she was looking for?

Suddenly she thought of another name she did remember. "Do you know the vet's assistant, Manny...somebody?"

The cowboy eyed her warily. "Yes'um. He's down to the stud barn just now. Would you like me to fetch him for you?"

The situation was getting worse and worse. Why hadn't she thought this through before she'd jumped into action? How would she find Witt when she had no idea what name he used?

"I..." she stammered.

"¿Qué paso, amigo? Something wrong?"

Carley spun in the direction of the familiar voice coming from behind her. She thought she'd armed herself with knowledge. But nothing could have prepared her for the sight of the man who'd haunted her dreams day and night, as he sauntered across the dirt in their direction.

"Thank God..." Her knees buckled and the next thing she knew Witt had her in his arms, holding her against his body for support.

She'd given up on ever feeling Witt's arms around her again. Months ago Carley had truly lost all hope. And now that she could feel his muscles rippling under her grip, could smell his own beloved musky scent as he held her near, the hope flared.

Witt stared down at her in his arms as if he was holding a complete stranger. The flame of hope quickly died again.

"Feeling all right, ma'am? You delirious or dehydrated, maybe? Being out here in the sun without a hat isn't too smart." He set her unsteadily on her feet and backed away—leaving one hand on her elbow for support. "How about if I take you back to the main house? Maybe a glass of water will help?"

Her parched body desperately needed to drink in the sight of him. She'd been thirsty for his embrace for far too long.

Reality splashed her like a cold shower. Nothing would help. Witt's first sight of her had not stirred any memories—in him.

Unfortunately, the sight of him brought stunning images crashing in on Carley. She fought the tantalizing memory of his kiss, so full of irresistible passion and erotic hunger. Her head swam with remembering his touch on her skin—the touch that could heat the blood in her veins and send shivers dancing down her spine. A fierce craving to draw them both into the inner fire nearly brought her to her knees for the second time since getting an initial glimpse of him after all these months.

"You need my help, Houston?" The ranch hand's question broke into her daydream.

Witt turned to the other man but moved his steadying hand to Carley's shoulder. "Naw. You go on back to work, pal. I think I can handle things here."

Witt eyed her with a sideways glance. "I can handle you, can't I, little lady?" He bent to whisper in her ear and the feel of his warm breath on her cheek suddenly seemed comforting.

For one fleeting moment Carley wondered if Witt could be faking a memory loss. But within an instant she knew, deep inside her bones, that the man she'd loved could not disguise his real identity—at least, not while he stood so close. When she didn't respond, his eyes narrowed to slits. He firmly gripped her elbow, leading her to the main house.

"Oh, Wi—" no sense confusing him by calling him a name he would likely not recognize "—cowboy," she choked. "I imagine you can handle me just fine."

If I can manage to control myself around you.

By the time Witt ushered her into the kitchen of the main house, Carley had regained, at least, partial control of her emotions. First things first. She needed to address him by a name that wouldn't be disorienting.

When he handed her a glass of water, she noticed her hands were shaking, but decided to ignore them.

"The name's Carley," she said, with more emphasis than necessary. "Carley Mills. What's yours?"

"Carley?" He took her free hand in both of his. "Nice name for such a dainty lady."

He grinned at her and she smiled back, not feeling the least bit happy.

"I'm known as Houston...Houston Smith, ma'am. I kinda run the ranch operation around here. You know...the horses and cattle?"

He'd suddenly spoken with cool politeness. She sensed it was as if he'd just remembered that strangers could mean trouble...even "dainty" strangers. His wary distance shattered her heart.

Would she be able to keep herself from pouring pent up desires and dreams all over him?

"And just what brings such a delicate flower to our little corner of Texas, Carley?" He released her hand and motioned for her to take one of the twelve chairs at the wooden kitchen table.

"I'm hardly what one might call *delicate*... Houston." She continued to stand but swallowed a big gulp of water to soothe her raspy throat. It didn't help. She was feeling dizzy, shaky and...delicate. Darn it.

At well over five-eight and a former world-class swimmer, *delicate* and *dainty* had never before been words used to describe her. But just now she felt weak-kneed and small.

"I've come to Casa de Valle to take over the psychologist's job while he's on temporary leave," she managed past the huge lump in her throat.

"You're a head doctor?"

"I have a doctorate in child psychology, yes."

"Should I call you Dr. Carley?"

"Some people address me as Doctor, but I'd prefer you call me Carley."

"I see. But what were you doing out in the—"

Houston was interrupted by a young girl's voice coming from the hallway. "Miz Mills?" The teenager appeared in the kitchen doorway carrying the one-year-old, currently whiny, Cami. "Oh, there you are, ma'am."

When Cami recognized her mother, she started to shriek. "Ma...Ma...Yeee!"

Carley pulled her daughter from the teenager's arms. "Hush, baby. Mama's right here."

"I'm sorry, Miz Mills. I tried to put her down for

a nap, but she wouldn't have any part of it. Then she started to cry and I couldn't find anything to make her happy.'' In Carley's professional opinion, the round-faced girl appeared to be feeling guilty.

"Don't worry about it, Rosie. It's just the new place and strange people. You didn't do anything wrong.'' Carley wiped a few crocodile tears from Cami's cheeks, but nothing she did consoled her daughter. "I'm sure she'll adjust just fine after a few days. Until then, don't hesitate to bring her to me if she seems distraught.''

"Yes'um. I gotta get back now. You want me to take her again?'' The earnest young girl looked panicked at the thought but was brave enough to ask.

"No, thanks.'' Carley found herself nearly shouting over Cami's cries. "Tomorrow is soon enough for a repeat performance. I'll keep her with me for now.''

Rosie beamed with relief and beat a hasty retreat.

Carley inspected Cami until the toddler became uncomfortable with the perusal and buried her face in her mother's shoulder, still sobbing and heaving heavy sighs. Carley patted her daughter's back and stroked Cami's hair as she turned to the man who'd been so silent through the whole scene. He looked rather shell-shocked.

"Anything wrong, Houston?'' Carley tensed in anticipation. Witt had never seen his daughter before— hadn't even known of her existence before his disappearance, but Cami's resemblance to him was unmistakable. Had he suddenly noticed? Had the sight of his daughter triggered some inner memory?

Two

The man who used to be Witt Davidson drawled a question in his languid, Texas accent. "That your daughter?"

"Yes. Her name is Camille. I named her after your—her grandmother. Her father's mother." Carley always wondered what Witt would say the first time he saw their daughter.

"Another pretty name for another pretty little thing."

That wasn't the way her dreams had gone. "Thank you. We call her Cami." Carley did her best to hold back the burning tears suddenly welling at the corners of her eyes.

With the first sound of Witt's voice, Cami had quieted. Now, at the mention of her name, Cami raised her head to stare at the new person making the baritone sounds. When she spotted him, her whole face lit up. She pointed a finger in his direction. "Da!"

Carley grabbed Cami's hand and held it to her chest. "Don't point, sweetie. It's not polite."

Houston Smith narrowed his eyes and studied the baby who was inspecting him with matching intensity. Something about this woman's child seemed familiar.

During the long months he'd lived in the Rio Grande Valley he'd learned to cope with the distressing feeling that everything, and everyone, seemed somehow familiar. But the sensation was particularly strong with Carley Mills and her baby.

As Gabe and Doc Luisa had kindly pointed out, a man without a past might easily mistake an enemy for a friend. He couldn't imagine Carley being an enemy, but everything was not as it appeared with her, either.

After all, what was a refined and citified-looking woman doing at a children's home in rural South Texas? The suit she wore probably cost more than she'd make working here in six months. And then there was the matter of her being out in the yard in the middle of the day, dressed to kill and without an obvious purpose.

Still…Houston was strangely drawn to her. When he'd put his arm around her shoulders to steady her, he'd felt a searing heat. Her nearness caused his flesh to jump, and he had a nearly uncontrollable urge to drag her against his chest and smother her with kisses.

He'd controlled his urges with a powerful effort. He'd been so careful up to now. So watchful all this time. His condition, when Dr. Luisa found him close to death and dumped along the side of a farm road, led both of them to believe someone had meant to finish the job and kill him. If that were true, somewhere in the world someone might still be after him. Was it possible this woman was a threat to him?

The baby raised her arms toward him. "Up. Pick me...me...now."

Carley tried to grab her daughter's attention. "No, honey. The man can't hold you right now. You mustn't beg strangers to pick you up, Cami. It could be dangerous."

Houston smiled at the baby, but there was no way he was touching that kid. She made him uncomfortable without his really knowing why.

Carley turned to him, an embarrassed smile on her face. "Sorry. She's usually timid around people she's never seen before. I do thank you for quieting her down, though. I'd hate having to wait for her to be still on her own." She scrutinized him with an unsettling gaze. "You must be good with kids."

"No." He backed up a step and changed the focus of the conversation. "The baby sure does look like you. Especially when she smiles."

"You think so? Most people say she's the spitting image of her father. Except for the eyes, of course."

Yes. Both the females in front of him had the same exotic shade of green eyes, the same slightly slanted looks when they gazed in his direction. But he could see that the child didn't carry the mother's complexion or hair coloring. And he couldn't imagine that smattering of freckles adorning the baby's nose ever marring the perfect face of the woman who held her.

In fact, something about the baby gave him the same eerie feeling he'd gotten when looking in a mirror. She sort of looked like the strange reflection he'd been seeing gazing back at him. But his own face was so unfamiliar he figured her resemblance must be his mind playing tricks on him. A few moments later he was sure of it.

"Where is the baby's father?" he blurted out before thinking. "Sorry. I didn't mean to be rude. You don't owe me any explanations."

He turned to the door, halting when the same old ache stabbed at his temple. Fighting the urge to rub his hand against the pain, he squeezed his eyes shut for a second instead. Would these headaches never go away?

Carley laid a hand on his arm. "Are you okay? You weren't being rude. That's a perfectly natural question."

She shifted the baby to her other arm. Houston could see she was tiring, but he'd be damned if he would offer to hold her child. He'd never held a baby. At least, he didn't think he had. And he certainly wasn't about to start with one who could make him feel so strange and disoriented.

Cami looked right into his soul—and he had no idea what she'd find there.

"Cami's father disappeared before she was born. He doesn't even know about her."

There were those tears again. The same ones he'd glimpsed the first time she'd made a remark about the baby's father. Houston reached for her face before he could think about what he was doing. He stroked his thumb lightly under her lashes to brush away a tear. When he felt her satiny skin beneath his fingers, the intimate friction excited him, made him want to grab her tightly and...

What in God's name was he thinking? Houston

jerked his hand away but continued standing there studying her.

Her eyes had widened at his touch, and she looked like a frightened little rabbit. He figured someone had hurt her badly. He suspected it was the baby's father. *Disappeared* was the word she'd used. Was that a polite word for *ran off?*

Houston Smith couldn't imagine a more cowardly act, or any reason on earth that might drag *him* away from a woman who looked as good as this one did. He hoped someday to come across the bastard who'd run off and left a beautiful, pregnant wife. Houston had a few things to teach him.

The more he gazed at her standing there, holding the now quiet child to her breast, the more he had to fight the urge to take them both in his arms while he placed a searing kiss on the mother's delectable lips. Whew. Where did that come from? Maybe it was the heat.

For a moment he'd thought…he'd imagined…

The crack of the screen door slamming behind his back made him snap to attention. But before he turned to the sound, he saw Carley tense and stiffen her spine. All of a sudden the frightened rabbit was gone. Something in her eyes went taut, and he caught a steel-edged toughness that he'd missed until now.

No question. His first hunch must have been right on target. There was more to this lady than met the eye.

Dr. Luisa Monsebais stepped into the kitchen and strolled to Houston's side with her usual familiar ease. The doctor might have gray hair and wrinkles on her face, but she was as spry and agile as a teenager.

"Everything going okay here?"

"Howdy, Doc. Sure thing. I've been getting acquainted with our newest employee." He turned to Carley and the baby, urging them forward to greet the crotchety, sharp-eyed woman who'd just come through the screen door.

"Dr. Carley Mills, meet Dr. Luisa Monsebais, the ranch's favorite pediatrician."

Luisa found her voice first. "Doctor?"

"Ph.D. in child psychology, Dr. Monsebais. I'm here to relieve Dan Lattimer, who's taken a personal leave."

Luisa stuck a hand in Carley's direction, but her sun-spotted face never crinkled into a smile. "Call me Luisa. Did Houston say your first name was Carley?"

Carley nodded and took Luisa's hand, but Houston noted that her solemn face held no welcome, either.

Their terse exchange might have made the women uncomfortable, but whatever bothered them didn't seem to include him. Their problem broke the clutch of tension that had gripped Houston since the baby's first appearance in the kitchen. Luisa's steady presence always calmed him when things became oppressive.

Luisa wrapped her arm around Houston's and spoke to him with twinkling eyes. "You taking the afternoon off?"

Houston grimaced. Trust Luisa to cut to the practical. Every move she'd made since she'd found him, unconscious and bleeding alongside the deserted levee road, had been logical and utilitarian.

He had no memory of Luisa finding him. In fact, no memory of anything before he awoke in her guest bedroom ten days later. It was two more weeks after that before he could think through the haze of pain long enough to question what had befallen him and why.

Doc Luisa had made the decision to bring him to her little home clinic instead of the nearby hospital. When he'd finally asked, she'd explained about his gunshot wounds and the empty ankle holster she'd found. This close to the border, her first assumption had been that he was some kind of drug runner or smuggler and wanted by the sheriff. But with his life hanging in the balance, she hadn't been able to face turning him over to the authorities. She'd figured if he were to die, there would be plenty of time for all the questions and forms.

Luisa told Houston that by the time it was clear he would live it was also clear he had no memory of his life before the incident—and she'd grown fond of him. Fond enough to persuade him not to seek information about his obviously dubious past—and to help him get on the road to a new life.

Houston was grateful as hell to Doc Luisa. With her gentle probing, he'd managed some snatches of memories about a childhood on a ranch. He remembered enough of a background working with animals so she could find him this job at the children's home—starting over, fresh and clean.

Luisa convinced Gabe Diaz, the old man who ran this foster home, to hire him without references. Gabe was the only other person alive who knew Houston couldn't remember a thing, and it was Gabe who'd managed the phony paperwork for his new identity. Good thing the man had a soft heart.

At this point Gabe and Luisa were all Houston had.

They'd saved him, protected him and befriended him. And he'd do the same for them.

For a few seconds Houston narrowed his gaze on the woman holding her child. Should he be wary of Carley? Could she be a threat to Gabe or Luisa—or him?

"Well, son? Is today a holiday I missed?"

He could feel his face flush as he grinned at the kindly but stern doctor. "No, ma'am. I'll be getting on back to work now." Houston turned from Luisa and addressed Carley as he touched a hand to the brim of his work hat. "Glad you're going to be around the ranch for a while, ma'am. But from now on, I'd stay out of the sun on hot afternoons if I were you."

Houston slammed through the screen door and out into that bright sun, all the while wondering how long the two strong-headed females he'd left standing in the kitchen would be civil to one another. And whether Carley Mills would be as much of a danger to his emotional and physical well-being as she'd already been to his hormones.

Man was she a looker! With all that mahogany-red hair, the olive complexion and those exotic green eyes, he was positive she must be the most luscious thing he'd ever encountered. She even smelled good enough to eat. The fragrance that seemed to belong to her alone was familiar, like over-ripe strawberries, but with a silken muskiness that captured his attention and made her special.

He headed back to work puzzling over the strong impression that he'd met her before. His mouth seemed to know the feel of her lips when they'd never touched them, his hands the feel of her skin in places he'd never even seen. But were those real memories…or just wishful thinking?

Carley stared through the screen door as the long, lanky cowboy strode across the yard, his boots kicking up little dust devils with every stride. She had to fight off the violent need to run after him. Her heart had wanted to beg him to stay and talk to her…for only a few minutes longer.

The sight of the dimple in his cheek when he grinned, the lock of sandy-blond hair that fell over one eyebrow even with his hat on and those pale-blue eyes that darkened to gray when he was disturbed thrilled her. The vulnerability she found in him made her want to gather him up and hold him close until he had no choice but to remember her.

"Our Houston's a special fellow, don't you think?"

The doctor's question disrupted Carley's daydream. She turned to face the older woman. "Special?" Carley bit her lip. "Yes, I do. Definitely."

Cami picked that minute to raise her head and rub an eye with her fist.

Doc Luisa squinted at the baby's face. "That a new enrollee at the ranch? I don't recognize her."

"This is my daughter, Cami. She'll be living here with me."

"Hmm. Doesn't resemble you much, does she?"

Carley felt a bead of sweat forming above her lip. "She has my eyes."

The older woman's deep-set, dark eyes held hers for a few seconds, then her face broke into a thousand creases as she bestowed a smile on the baby and her mother. The angle of her head told Carley that she'd come to some decision about them. But Carley didn't care to discuss anything with Doc Luisa or anybody else just yet. First she needed to get to a phone.

"I'd better put Cami down for a nap. We've both had a long day."

"You came in this morning? Where'd you come from?"

Carley moved Cami from one hip to the other. "Houston. It's a longer drive than I thought."

The doctor chuckled. "A long drive full of mesquite and cactus…and not much else. You from the city?"

"I've been living there for a few years, but I was born in South Carolina, raised in New Orleans."

Luisa's eyes sparkled with intelligence and a secret mirth all their own. "Born in Charleston, I'd wager."

"Well, yes." Carley wanted to be away from this woman who was too quick—too smart. "I really need to get Cami upstairs. If you'll excuse me?" All Carley wanted right this minute was that phone.

Doc Luisa laid a staying hand on Carley's arm. "Go on for now. But we will talk, young woman. I think you have quite a few things to explain." Luisa glanced over to Cami who was about to screw her face up for a good tantrum. "I'm here at the ranch every morning to check on the kids. Only reason I'm so late today is I stopped to look in on a child with a lingering case of measles."

Cami's pout turned into a whine, but the doctor still held on to Carley's arm. "That young man means the world to me. I wouldn't take kindly to anyone who thought to hurt him." She narrowed her eyes and made sure Carley understood her change of topic.

Carley understood perfectly.

* * *

Carley climbed the carpeted stairs leading from the front hall to the employees' bedrooms and lounge area. Where the downstairs living and sleeping rooms were typically institutional, with linoleum floors and sturdy metal or plastic furniture, the upstairs wing was tastefully decorated and homey.

Well, okay, the walls appeared in need of a coat of paint, and the carpet had worn spots with a few frays around the edges—but everything was spotless. The warm woods of the floors and furniture were polished to a high, glossy gleam. The place reminded Carley of her grandfather's house in New Orleans—right down to the smell of lemon oil and vanilla.

When she carried Cami into their room, Carley noticed someone had put fresh flowers on her dresser and had made up both the double bed and the roll-away crib. Grateful for the reprieve from homemaking duties, she lowered Cami into the crib and whispered a few soothing words, hoping she'd close her eyes for a rest.

The poor little tyke was so overtired she barely had the energy to cry. But cry she did—as if her heart were breaking.

Carley pulled open the diaper bag and hauled out a change of clothes, diapers and a half-size baby bottle. She changed Cami and went into the bathroom to fill the bottle with water. When she returned, Carley nearly stumbled over the open bag. She heard a clink and remembered that she'd crammed her framed photograph of Witt into the side pocket.

Of course! No wonder Cami seemed to recognize the man. Carley had kept his picture on her dresser for all these months. Smart kid. Houston Smith was no stranger to her. In fact, Carley had told her over and over that he was her daddy. No doubt Cami was brokenhearted because the man she thought of as "daddy" had not recognized her.

Carley gave Cami the bottle of water and her favorite stuffed toy, a pink crayfish that Carley's mother had given her. Before long, sleep closed the baby's eyes and quieted her sobs.

Carley knew she'd better not keep Witt's picture in plain sight here at the ranch, so she buried it inside one of her suitcases for storage. Then she reached for the mobile phone she'd also stuffed in the pocket of the diaper bag.

Slightly warm in the closed room, Carley pulled open the window, then punched in the many numbers necessary to reach Reid Sorrels. A hot, stiff breeze blasted her as it came from off the range, and she took a deep breath as Reid answered her call.

Before saying hello, he spat the question at her. "Is it Davidson?"

"You knew all the time it was. But, yes, I can confirm he's Witt." She gave her boss a pithy statement of what she'd found, then cut to what she needed from him.

"Run complete backgrounds on a local pediatrician, Dr. Luisa Monsebais, and on the home's administrator, Gabriel Diaz. See if you can get hard copies to me without anyone knowing."

"They'll arrive in the local field office no later than tomorrow. Someone will get them to you on the ranch." Reid fell silent for a minute. "He didn't recognize you at all?"

"Not that I could tell. It's so strange here, Reid.

Otherworldly. And what with Witt being this Houston Smith person, I feel cut off and alone.''

' ''Try plugging your laptop into the Bureau's satellite link. Maybe you'll be in range there. And check in with me twice a day by phone.''

Carley smiled grimly at Reid's no-nonsense reply, but she wasn't through with her requests. ''Contact a Dr. William Fields at the Cannon Neurological Institute in Chicago and arrange for a conference call today. Both of us need to pick his brain on this one.'' She stared absently out the open window at the scruffy live oaks and prickly ebony trees. ''Call me back when you've reached him. I'll wait here.''

Carley cut the connection and cradled the instrument against her breast. Reid had bent the rules for Witt. By all rights, he should have picked Witt up and carted him off in custody to interrogation the first moment Manny had ID'd him. But Reid waited for her report—and now he'd wait a little longer.

Witt had been one of the best agents on the task force. His loss set the operation back years, and his unexplained disappearance caused a black mark against Reid. Not to mention the fact that Reid had unfortunately lost her, in a way, to the same calamity: Carley had spent months searching fruitlessly for word of Witt among the lowlife gathering spots and bars near Houston where they'd been investigating the kidnapping ring. She'd researched Witt's background, even visiting the little town in West Texas where he'd grown up.

Digging further, she'd located his former teachers, the grave sites of his family and talked to some old neighbors and friends. All the checking gave her a better picture of the man who'd disappeared—but didn't give her the man.

Carley found that he'd been scarred in many ways because of his childhood. She'd worked with children from similar backgrounds, children who'd shut off their emotions rather than take a chance on being hurt again. Many turned into adults afraid to commit, afraid to trust.

Because his mother had died early and his abusive father had been killed in a drunken rage, Witt might never have been able to give her the love she craved. But she'd been sure he was a responsible and honorable man who would never just deliberately disappear. Still, he was gone without a trace.

As the time neared for Cami to be born, the doctors had ordered Carley to bed. She'd collapsed with exhaustion and despair.

Cami's birth had rallied Carley's spirit. Her little girl was a constant reminder of the man she loved. Carley knew that as long as she and Cami were together, they'd someday find the answers. She never gave up on finding him. Never.

But now she wanted to know what had happened to keep him from her that night eighteen months ago. How he'd lost his memory, and what had become of him during the unaccounted month when he'd first disappeared.

She figured the man calling himself Houston Smith was the only one who could give her all the answers. But Carley needed to find a way to help him remember—and to bring Witt back to her.

The conference call came through two hours later.

Dr. Fields took the time for explanations. In the end, his descriptions were thorough, if not hopeful.

"Please, Doctor," she begged. "We can give you a couple of hypothetical causes for the amnesia. Can't you give us some possibilities?"

After a long-winded, ten-minute lecture on one possible cause, Reid broke into the doctor's explanation. "Hold it. I need a translator."

"The doctor's simply saying that a person can have something so horrible happen to him that his mind refuses to acknowledge it," Carley explained to her boss. "Sometimes the person might even blank out not only the terrible event but also everything that came before."

Carley tried to make the doctor spell out that kind of malfunction for Reid's benefit. "This would be more a psychiatric problem, wouldn't it Dr. Fields?"

"Indeed, but it would be recognized under the branch of medicine called cognitive neuropsychology. Unfortunately, for the condition to continue for a period of eighteen months would, by definition, mean the person had immersed himself in a drastic, multiple-personality disorder that would take literally years of intense therapy to conquer."

The idea of Witt having such a dire mental illness made Carley shudder. "Let's hope that's not the case here. What if it was not the denial of an event but rather an actual physical trauma that's caused this amnesia?"

"That's the other possibility. Any trauma to the head can cause brain damage, bruising the cerebral cortex and causing problems with memory retrieval. I would naturally need to study the brain scans before I could attempt to assess the extent of such damage."

Carley was getting impatient with the doctor's

hedging. "Yes, but can't you tell us *in general* the symptoms and recovery time?"

After a few seconds of indignant silence, the doctor continued. "Brain trauma can cause temporary loss of personal memories...for instance, one's identity, while other memories like language skills and word recognition that are stored in a different part of the brain are not lost."

"Right. I've seen movies where this happens." Reid sounded as eager to get to the point as Carley felt. "But those memories do come back, don't they?"

"Normally, following trauma, patients have what are called 'islands of memory.' These isolated events can act as anchors for memory recovery. In most cases, all old memories, except for the actual trauma itself, are recovered. It's conceivable, though, that large areas of memory will be permanently irretrievable."

"What?" Reid sounded stunned. "Carley, is he saying that Davidson may never remember who he is or what happened to him?"

"Shh, Reid. Let the doctor finish, then we'll discuss this rationally." Carley was amazed her voice seemed so calm when inside she was a mass of nerve endings. "Would it do any good in such a case to force the person to try to remember, Dr. Fields? Or to try something drastic like hypnosis or drugs, perhaps?"

"Absolutely not. Any further emotional or physical shock could cause the victim's memories to retreat even further. No, the best course of action is to provide a safe environment where familiar things can be introduced slowly. If the patient inquires about his past, do not lie or confuse the issue, but gently steer him toward self-revelation.''

Carley thanked the specialist for his time, clicked him off and tried to placate Reid. Her boss was chomping at the bit to bundle Witt up and drag him off to an institution for examination and second opinions, exactly as she'd feared.

She managed to dissuade Reid by begging for some time to ease herself into Witt's trust. Carley figured once Houston Smith trusted her, getting his memory back might come along naturally with the familiarity between them.

Finally Reid calmed enough to foresee the dangers he'd missed before. ''I'm sorry I got you and Cami into this. I'd imagined that when you showed up, Witt would see you and remember everything. Guess that's not going to happen. What do you want to do now?''

She couldn't believe he would even need to ask the question. ''Why, stay with him, of course.''

Reid's voice softened when he said, ''Carley, he has another life now. What if it takes a year…two…or more?''

''I'll be here to help him, no matter how long it takes.''

Her boss lowered his tone to where she could barely hear him. ''What if he never remembers you?''

For a moment she hesitated, but every strand of human frailty that held her to this unjust planet screamed the same answer throughout her body. ''Then we'll just have to make new memories,'' she whispered. ''I believe he loved me once. Deep down he's the same person. With enough time, perhaps he'll grow to love me again.''

''Sorry, Charleston. I can only give you a couple

more weeks.'' Reid's voice had grown strong and professional once more.

"Being without Davidson has been a challenge," he added. "Having to do without you, as well, would be more than the operation can stand."

"Only a couple of weeks?"

"That's more than I should give you. In the meantime, watch your back...and his. Whoever or whatever caused this amnesia is bound to come back sooner or later to finish the job. You want to stay there with him for a few weeks? Okay. But you're totally responsible for his welfare. In his condition, he's completely defenseless."

Three

Fifteen minutes and dozens of instructions later, Carley snapped closed her mobile phone and took a deep breath. Reid had agreed to wait and to let her and Cami stay on the ranch—for now. But that wasn't her biggest worry.

Despite what she'd told Reid, deep inside she was frozen with the fear that perhaps Witt would never remember. What if she never again felt his warm breath on her cheek or thrilled to the electric shock of having his body pulled tightly against hers?

Hearing herself make a noise somewhere between a muffled sob and a sigh, Carley fought the lump forming deep in her throat. At that moment another tiny sob penetrated the stillness of the dusty sunset pouring through the open window.

Carley spun to see Cami standing in the crib, onc

hand holding the rail and the other fisted in her mouth.

Silent, sad eyes stared at Carley through the shadows of the room. "Mama…home?"

Carley crossed the room and picked up her sleepy-eyed child. "Oh, baby," she crooned, as she bent her head to gently kiss the soft, fuzzy cap of straw-colored curls. "It looks like this is home for a while. We're just going to have to make the best of it."

A quiet knock disturbed Carley's reverie as she stood in the middle of the room, gently swaying back and forth, patting Cami's flannel covered back.

"Yes?"

"Miz Mills?" The door inched open enough to allow Rosie, the teenage caretaker, to stick her head in the room. When she saw Carley holding the baby, she stepped further inside. "Preacher Gabe said to tell you the senior staff's supper hour is at seven o'clock."

Cami turned from her mother's shoulder to gaze at the intruder. When Rosie spotted Cami, Carley was amazed to see the short, dark-haired teenager grinning back at her daughter.

"Um. Do you think maybe Cami would give me another chance to be friends?" Rosie took a step in their direction.

Carley couldn't help but smile. "You'll have to ask Cami. But she has a forgiving nature. And I think she and I both could stand to have a new friend right now."

Rosie's chocolate-colored eyes turned serious, but she forced a smile as she held her arms out to entice Cami to come to her. "Want to be my friend, Cami?"

Cami gazed silently at the young woman for a moment, then turned to get a hint from her mother. Carley knew her approval was crucial, so she smiled at both of them.

"It's okay, Cami. Rosie is our friend."

Cami's face broke into a big grin and she nearly flung herself from her mother's arms into the waiting arms of the surprised teenager.

Carley gathered up some of Cami's things. "Would you like to feed her dinner and sit with her while I eat, Rosie?"

The girl nodded as she brushed Cami's wispy strands into some semblance of order.

"Good. That'll give me a chance to get to know…"

The roar of an engine blasted through the quiet twilight on the range, completely drowning out Carley's words. Her body went wire tight as she stepped to the window. Through the trees, Carley caught a glimpse of a man on a motorcycle, spinning circles in the dirt of the barnyard.

To her horror a horse and its rider picked that exact moment to ride into view. When the horse spied the motorcycle, it shied back and tried to turn. The cowboy held on and refused to let the poor, scared animal have its way. Finally the horse reared up, adding its own complaint to the gunning sounds of the motorcycle.

Carley barely had time to fuss over the treatment of the horse when its rider's hat went flying. She froze. There on the back of a bucking animal bent on destruction was Witt.

My God. "No more physical traumas," the doctor had said. And Reid had warned her that she was responsible.

For heaven's sake, get off that horse!

While curtailing the hysterical scream threatening to explode from her throat, Carley threw a couple of choked instructions over her shoulder to Rosie. Flying down the stairs, she pushed through the kitchen door to the yard. Her body's jangled nerves energized her steps with a desperate need to keep Houston safe.

The screen door slammed open and snapped back, catching her heel. She cussed under her breath but kept on moving past the trees that shaded the house and temporarily obscured her view of the yard.

After clearing the trees, she came to an abrupt halt. There in the center of the open space stood Houston Smith, holding the reins of a quieted horse with one hand while he slapped his hat against the jeans covering his massive thigh with the other. And he was smiling. Smiling and chatting with the fellow clad totally in leather who'd just shut down the powerful engine of his motorcycle.

She picked up her pace again and raced to the middle of the expanse of dirt. The smell of sweaty animal mingled with the pungent odor of motorcycle exhaust made her wish for a fresh breath of air.

Within a few feet of the men, she had to hockey-stop before plowing right into Houston. "What in the hell do you think you're doing?"

"Ma'am?"

He turned around, and Carley felt a sucker punch to her gut. His gaze was wary and confused. Not at all the look she was used to getting from her lover. All these lonely, desperate months she'd dreamed of that cocky grin and the sexy inspection he usually bestowed upon her. Now, here he was, only a few feet away, and he practically looked right through her.

"You might have been killed. You shouldn't be riding a horse." She sucked in a breath and tried to stem the shakes causing her voice to quiver. "Stick to walking and cars, why don't you?"

"Ma'am?" His eyes took on a rather quizzical, dancing quality, as if he suddenly found her quite amusing.

She'd be amusing, all right. If he didn't quit calling her ma'am, she might have to ignore the doctor's orders and punch him right in that gorgeous, grinning mouth. How was she supposed to explain to him why he had to be careful—why another blow to the head might kill any chance for him to remember his past life—his past love?

"Uh. You were too rough on the horse. He almost threw you. You're too important to the ranch to be doing anything so dangerous."

"Ma'am?" This time the tone of his voice was more than casual but less than cordial.

She ground her teeth and stepped closer to him. "Stop saying that. I'm only trying to make you think about being more careful, that's all."

A roar of raucous laughter erupted behind her. She spun to face the other man, still seated on the chrome and black motorcycle. His eyes were covered by reflector-type, aviator sunglasses, and he was grinning widely.

"I think that's a slam aimed at your horsemanship, *amigo*." The dark-skinned man removed his glasses and aimed a decidedly sexual ogle in Carley's direction. He let his gaze wander slowly down her face, across her chest and linger around her hips. "You want to warn me about the dangers of a motorcycle, sugar?"

She sniffed once, raised her chin and turned back to the cowboy with the horse. "Look, I..."

"No, you look...*ma'am.*" Houston's eyes glinted the color of iron in the shadows of the setting sun. "I don't know what you thought you saw, or why you thought it concerned you, but I was definitely not too rough on this horse. And I was not about to be thrown."

She felt her eyes widen at his sharp tone. Just when she thought she'd better devise some lie to cover her behavior, his eyes softened and his mouth curled up in a semblance of a smile.

"You know much about horses? Ever ridden one?"

"Me? No, but..."

Houston slid the Stetson on his head and pulled down the brim to partially cover his eyes. "Well, now. I'd say that's an oversight we should do something about. I think a riding lesson might be just what you need to be more comfortable around the ranch."

"I don't think so." She gulped. "In fact, I was about to suggest you start doing your work from the front seat of a truck. They do use trucks on modern ranches, don't they?"

He chuckled and reached around to pat the nose of his horse. "No call to be afraid of horses. Take Poncho here, for instance." Houston continued to stroke the horse's neck. "He'll work as hard as any man for however long you ask of him, and with barely a sign of complaint."

"Only if you treat him right." The man on the motorcycle, with jet-black eyes matching his shoulder-length hair, cut in. "And Houston Smith is better to his animals than any man on earth."

Carley faced the man still astride his bike.

"There's no need to concern yourself with Houston's welfare, miss. The horses respect his authority and his attention. They know he'd die before he'd let anything bad happen to them."

That's just what she was afraid of.

Houston cleared his throat with what she sensed was embarrassment. "Uh. Carley, have you met our veterinarian's assistant, Manny Sanchez?"

Manny Sanchez, the FBI undercover agent.

Carley felt her old dauntlessness returning, and her feet were suddenly back on solid ground. She bestowed a sultry grin on the jaunty, windblown man astride the bike while he showed a typical interest in her sexual overture.

She also delighted in watching his eyes change expression when she purred in her best Southern accent, "Pleased to meet you, Manny. My name's Carley Mills and I think we have a mutual friend...Reid Sorrels from Houston. You remember him, don't you, sugar?"

Manny's shoulders straightened, and he swung his leg over the motorcycle. He practically stood at attention when he faced her. "Carley? You're Carley Mills?" He flicked a glance between Carley and the man still holding the reins of his horse.

Carley was positively amused at the range of emotions that filtered across Manny's face before he found his professional mask. "Yeah. Y-yes, certainly," he stammered. "Reid Sorrels. How is good ol' Reid, anyway?"

"Last time I saw him he was quite well," she purred with a smile. "I would imagine, though, that he'd appreciate hearing from you. You should give him a call sometime.''

''Uh, yeah. I'll do that.'' He shifted his stance to address the other man. ''I'd better be going, Houston. I'll see you first thing in the morning.''

''You bet.'' Houston narrowed his eyes to appraise the tension he'd felt develop between Manny and Carley. ''Sure you can't stay for supper? Gabe's issued you an open invitation.''

''No, thanks. Some other time maybe.'' Manny mounted the saddle of his bike like he would a horse and slanted a quick glance in Carley's direction. ''Why don't you move Poncho back a few feet, Smith.''

Slightly surprised by Manny's seeming change of attitude, Houston tightened down his hold on the reins and clicked his tongue at Poncho. He'd moved several yards away when he heard the motorcycle rumble to life. Houston jerked his head around just in time to catch Manny and Carley in an animated conversation he couldn't hear.

A spurt of jealousy raced through his veins. He shook his head at the unwanted and unnecessary emotion. What was the matter with him? He'd only just met the woman this afternoon. True, she was undoubtedly the sexiest woman he could ever remember having seen, but that wasn't saying much, seeing as how his memory only extended back eighteen months.

He stood, stroked a hand down Poncho's muzzle and stared at Carley as she bent over to say something to Manny. She'd changed into jeans and a pullover shirt since the last time he'd seen her.

As Carley leaned, he noticed how long-legged she

was, and how the shirt she wore pulled above the waistband of her jeans, revealing a wide swath of silky, soft skin. His gaze drifted lower and landed on the firmness of her bottom. The jeans stretched tightly across the rounded contours of the flesh they contained.

Immediately hard and throbbing, he swallowed back the budding lust. No woman had done this to him since he'd awakened in Luisa's spare bed with more aches and pains than he'd thought possible to live through. Houston didn't know why this particular woman affected him so thoroughly—or so quickly. The ache he was experiencing surprised him, but made him feel more alive than at anytime during the past year and a half.

Carley smiled at Manny with some secret they'd just shared, and Houston had to clamp down on his rising anger. The urge to rip Manny off that motorcycle by the back of his neck and draw a little blood while he pasted a fist in the man's face rattled Houston.

Although he hadn't known him long, Manny had become one of his few friends. A good buddy to go have a long-neck with after work. And what of the woman? He barely knew her, and sure as heck didn't trust her.

Houston gritted his teeth and blew out a deep breath. Instead of punching someone, he lifted the Stetson and used his shirtsleeve to wipe away the perspiration dripping from his forehead. Dang. The muggy weather must have caused the pounding in his head to start up again.

Manny replaced his sunglasses, nodded in Houston's direction, gunned his machine and drove away.

Houston made a snap decision when Carley took a step toward him.

He simply nodded in her direction as Manny had done, tugged on Poncho's reins and walked away, too. No sense begging for trouble.

Sitting across from Carley at the dinner table was having a decidedly negative effect on Houston's mood. It hadn't put much of a damper on his appetite, but now that dinner was nearly over, he contemplated leaving before dessert.

He hadn't minded when the women at the table fawned over her. But as Carley gave each of them one of her room-brightening smiles, Houston's gut tightened in automatic reflex.

Then there were the men of the staff. Gabe, with a new haircut and spanking clean shirt, had held her chair for her. Frank Silva, head counselor, grabbed the chair next to hers and managed to brush their hands every time food needed to be passed. Even old Lloyd, the yellow-toothed cook, served Carley's meal first, then stood transfixed next to her place until the room erupted in laughter.

All in all, between the jalapeño pepper salad and the irritation over his unfathomable feelings for Carley, Houston had a lump in his stomach that wouldn't go away. Maybe he should leave. He figured he needed a little space to think over the day's events and their effect on him.

"Great meal, Lloyd," Carley crooned in that danged, Southern accent. Lloyd set a bowl of peach ice cream down in front of her and grinned like an adolescent while he absently wiped his hands on his apron.

She batted her eyelashes at him. "What herb did you use on the roasted chicken? It was wonderful."

"Aw. That there were just my rosemary chicken dish. Glad you liked it. Maybe I'll fix you something real special tomorrow night."

"My mother used to say that rosemary was the symbol for remembrance and fidelity," Gabe managed between bites.

Carley beamed at him, then sneaked a peek in Houston's direction. When she met his eyes, her grin faded and her whole face turned rather sad.

Well, that wasn't terribly ego boosting—or hopeful.

Frank Silva, who was well over forty and making a fool of himself, refused his dessert when Lloyd offered, turning instead to demand Carley's attention. "How'd your first day in the Rio Grande Valley go? Think you'll be able to settle in here?"

"I've never been anywhere quite like this. The scenery is so…flat. Are there any hills at all?"

Frank smiled and Houston noticed he'd slicked his hair across the bald spot in front. "Nope. Keep in mind this area used to be the flood plain for the Rio Grande. Though, since the dams upriver have been in place, the river's been tamed."

Frank covered Carley's hand with his own. "Besides the scenery, how are you taking to the people? Seen anyone you'd particularly like to get to know better?"

Houston nearly jumped out of his seat. It took all his willpower and Carley's own gentle freeing of her hand from Frank's grasp to keep Houston in place.

"Everyone's been so nice to us. I can't quite understand the language ya'll use, though. I don't believe I've ever heard anyone begin a sentence in Spanish then finish off in English before."

Everyone at the table chuckled and smiled at their new co-worker. Houston could only blankly stare at the top button of her crisp white blouse. It wasn't closed securely, and the tiny patch of skin revealed at the base of Carley's neck drew him like an ant to spilled sugar.

"It's called Tex-Mex, Carley," Gabe murmured. "Here on the border, lots of things are different from anywhere else." Gabe's eyes danced behind his wire-framed glasses.

"Excuse me, please."

All eyes at the table turned to the doorway. One of the teenage girls, Rosie, stood there, hesitating to enter the room full of adults. She was holding Carley's baby.

Carley jumped up and moved around the table. She took Cami from the girl's arms. "Everything okay, Cami?"

"Nothing's wrong, ma'am," the teenager quickly added. "It's almost curfew, though, and I was wondering if you wanted me to put Cami down for the night."

The whole table turned to Carley holding the baby in her arms. She swiveled so that Cami faced the room. "For all of you who haven't met her, this is my daughter, Cami."

The baby beamed down at the adults, who gaped at her.

"Excuse us a minute while I say good-night and give Rosie a couple of instructions." Carley smiled and shuttled the teenager and the baby out the door.

Houston glanced down at his spoon hovering over

the ice cream bowl. His appetite had sure disappeared now. Sensing the room was too quiet as he dropped the spoon against the dish, he looked up and every pair of eyes was locked on his face.

''What?'' Houston gulped. ''Did I do something wrong?''

Gabe cleared his throat. ''No, son, you didn't do anything wrong. It's getting late.'' He backed his chair away from the table and stood. ''I'd better have a word with Carley before I head on upstairs for the night.''

Over his shoulder, Gabe made one last remark to the cook. ''Great meal once again, Lloyd.''

Most of the other staff members took their cue from the boss, thanked Lloyd and stood to say good-night. Houston was still curious, but glad for the reprieve from all that attention. After standing and stretching his legs, Houston started after Gabe. He wanted to question him about the odd events at the table, but at that exact moment the screen door opened, and Doc Luisa stuck her head in through the doorway.

''Hey, there. Supper over?''

''Doc? What're you doing here at this hour? One of the kids sick?'' Houston asked.

Luisa stood on her tiptoes to place a kiss on his cheek. ''I just stopped by to say good-night to my favorite ex-patient, and to have a word with…Gabe.''

''You'd better hurry, then. Gabe just took off to speak to Carley and then go on up to bed.''

Houston picked his hat up off the counter and plopped it on his head. He needed a breath of air. ''Well, 'night, Doc.''

Luisa was half way across the kitchen headed toward Gabe's office. She waved a hand over her shoulder to him and disappeared around the corner.

People were sure behaving weirdly tonight, Houston thought as he closed the screen door behind him, shrugging his shoulders and brushing off the strange reactions. He had enough to occupy his mind without worrying about everyone else.

Stepping into the humid night air, he glanced up at the star-filled sky and wondered, not for the first time or the last, if somewhere someone was worried about him. Was there anyone out there who cared that he was missing?

Four

Carley crossed her legs and leaned back in one of the hard, wooden chairs in Gabe's office. She briefly considered how a misbehaving teenager would feel when faced with this kind of inquisition. Probably the same way she did now—uncomfortable.

Gabe ushered Luisa into another wooden chair and closed the door behind her. He eased himself behind the old, steel-case desk and into his leather rocker. Both he and Luisa sat stiffly while they studied Carley.

With a silent sigh Carley prepared herself to answer the questions she knew were coming—or at least some of them. She had a few questions of her own, and she intended to pose them before this inquest concluded.

Gabe began the interrogation. "Carley, what we discuss here need never leave this room, but I must insist that you be completely honest with us if we are going to keep you under our roof.''

"Cut to the chase," Luisa muttered, then forged ahead. "Is that baby really your daughter?" She pinned Carley with a steely stare, daring her to tell the truth.

"Yes, she is."

"And she's Houston's baby, too, isn't she?"

"Yes."

"How did you know where to find him?"

"A friend of a friend spotted him here and contacted me. Another friend got me the job."

"Hmm." Luisa rubbed her neck and relaxed into her chair. "I wondered if someone would come looking for him eventually. I never expected it to be the mother of his child."

"Are you really a child psychologist?" Gabe asked.

"Yes, certainly. I intend to fulfill the job you brought me here to do."

"You know he has amnesia?" When Carley nodded, Luisa narrowed her gaze and her mouth puckered in disdain. "Why haven't you told him who you are, or who the baby is?"

"He disappeared before Cami was born, so he wouldn't have any memories of her, anyway. And…I consulted with a top neuropsychologist. His recommendation is to guide Houston slowly to the brink of his memories. It could be dangerous to his mental health if we rush him or push him in any way."

"So your intention is to stick around until he remembers on his own? What if he never remembers you?"

Carley couldn't help but smile. This was the second

time someone had asked her that same question. Her answer remained unchanged.

"I love the man, Luisa. Now that I've found him, I'd never willingly walk away from him." Carley felt her face warm at the mention of their love. "Someday maybe he'll remember what we shared. If not, perhaps we can find some common ground to start over."

It was Gabe's turn to relax back into his chair. Apparently, Carley had answered all his questions satisfactorily.

Luisa was not so easily swayed, however. "Are there others who've been missing Houston? People who might want to come here to find him…like family, or employers?"

"He has no family except Cami. His employer knows where he is and is willing to wait and see whether Houston remembers or not."

Luisa waved a hand to cut through Carley's explanation. "Dang it, girl, you know what I'm asking. Was the man we know as Houston Smith a criminal in his past life? Is he wanted by the law somewhere?"

Carley couldn't keep the grin off her face. She'd been an undercover agent long enough to recognize innocent intent in people. If Gabe and Luisa thought Houston might be a criminal, then very likely they were not criminals themselves. Of course, that also meant they'd been harboring what they considered a potential felon. She shifted in her hard wooden chair and her smile dissolved.

"No. Houston is not, and never has been, a criminal." The time had come for some of Carley's questions. She sat up and narrowed her gaze at the two older people who faced her.

"Just how is it you two came across Houston Smith? Where did you find him?"

Carley also fancied herself a good judge of human nature. If either of these two tried to lie to her, she'd see through them in an instant.

Luisa answered her questions with a steady gaze and clear voice. "I found him beaten to a bloody pulp, shot and unconscious on a deserted road near here. I brought him to my clinic. I thought I was just going to make him comfortable...to die. But he's one tough case. Within ten days he started coming around. He never did remember what happened to him." She breathed a mournful sigh. "Just as well, I suppose."

Carley winced at the images of the man she loved broken and near death. "So you believe his amnesia was caused by the blows to his head?"

"Of course. What else? Actually, I'm surprised he's not blind, deaf and dumb as well," Luisa grumbled.

The frustration of not having known where he was and not being able to help him almost swamped Carley again—the same as it had when she'd been ordered to bed all those months ago. She fought it off now. He was alive and well, and she and Cami were here to make sure he was never alone again.

"And why didn't you notify the sheriff about him?" Carley sat back in her chair and narrowed her gaze at the two elderly people in front of her.

For the first time Luisa squirmed in her chair, and Gabe seemed to shrink into his.

"We...that is...I had grown so fond of the boy by the time I realized he would make it that I...well, dang it," Luisa began. "I figured he'd be wanted for something, and he'd already suffered so much.

What's the harm in allowing a man to begin anew? He didn't remember any of his past transgressions. Why make him face the consequences for acts he didn't recall?''

Carley's heart softened toward the elderly woman, whose gruff exterior hid her own soft nature. But there was more to be learned.

"Tell me more about the place where you found him," she probed.

Luisa studied her a minute. "Are we under interrogation here, young woman? You sound like you've questioned people before. Is there something you'd like to share with us?"

"You answer my questions first." Carley pinned the woman with her best steely look.

Luisa nodded her head slowly. "Okay...it was right before dawn. I'd just spent the night helping a migrant woman deliver her twins." She hesitated a second then continued. "They were camped down near the river. The Border Patrol found them and sent for me when they realized there wasn't time for anything else.

"Anyway, I took a shortcut down the levee road, but my headlights spotlighted a lump in my path. I figured it was an animal of some sort, but when I drove nearer and it hadn't moved I got out to investigate. When I saw what it really was, I figured he was dead. But he did still have a pulse. I dragged him into my car and gave him what comfort I could.''

"You didn't see anyone else? Find anything that might tell you what had happened to him?"

Luisa shrugged a shoulder. "Nope. Mind you, I didn't look much right then, I was a tad busy."

"He was shot, how about the bullet? Do you still have it?" Carley was grasping for any kind of clue.

"Bullet went right through. I did go back later…looking for his wallet or a…gun. I found nothing. As dry as it's been lately, you couldn't even tell a car had driven by in the last few months."

At Carley's silent contemplation, Luisa asked her own question. "You with the law someway, girl?"

Carley nodded slightly but had to tell her she wasn't at liberty to explain. She did assure both of them that the children would not be in any danger. Later, after she'd excused herself and gone upstairs to check on Cami, she stood at their bedroom window and stared out on the star brightened yard.

Oh, my love, how did you come to this strange place?

Carley wrapped her arms around herself and leaned her forehead against the glass window. For the thousandth time in the past eighteen months, she wished for things to be different. Why hadn't she told Witt about their baby when she had the chance? Why hadn't she made him admit his feelings for her?

She forced back the tears, remembering him in the clearing in the woods on that last fateful late-night sting. Laughing and so full of life, he told her he'd be back soon. Then he'd stepped away forever.

She rubbed at the tension in the back of her neck while she dreamed a different ending to the one reality had forced upon them. What if she'd asked him not to go after that truck he'd thought he'd seen? What if she'd begged him to stay with her? Where would they be right now?

Shaking the wishes from her cobwebbed brain, she turned her back on stars that never answered her pleas. It had been such an amazing day. The frustrating work of making the closed-off and distant Houston Smith learn to love again stretched before her like an endless highway. Could she make it happen in a couple of weeks?

Houston loved early mornings. The stillness brought silence and solitude, a respite from the terrors of the night and noisy business of the daylight hours.

He suppressed a chuckle as his boots clogged across the kitchen tile in the main house. Last night was different from all the rest. It wasn't fear that kept him awake. No, his sleeplessness began and ended with visions of the warm and sensual Carley.

Errant dreams still played with his mind. Dreams of Carley, wild and primitive, rising naked over him, pushing him past the rational world. She bit his neck and dug her fingernails into his shoulders in her passion.

Houston flexed his hands with the memory of driving them through her thick, rich hair. Only, it wasn't a real memory, even if it felt more real than anything else in his current life. It was only a dream.

Still half-aroused and wondering why his dreams of a woman he'd just met should seem so real, he tried to focus on the nightmares that had been intermingled with his sweet visions of Carley. Those dark and terrifying imaginings. The ones he'd thought he'd banished weeks ago. The quiet of the morning calmed him and made the dreams seem not so real.

Since he had no memories of childhood, family or fond friendships to guide his relationships with others, Houston genuinely liked to be alone. Single life meant no fear. No fear of whoever had stolen his memories, no fear of forgetting an enemy and no fear of remembering a broken heart. But at night, when the dark dreams came calling, wispy patches of dread held free rein and controlled his world.

Deep in his soul Houston knew he had not been a coward in his previous life. Even now, he'd rather face the truth head-on than hide…but what was the truth? And who could he trust?

Houston pulled a mug from the cabinet and poured himself a cup of the coffee Lloyd had made just before heading to the shower. In another half hour Lloyd would be throwing pots and pans around the kitchen while he performed his magic breakfast rituals.

By that time Houston's day would be in full swing, beginning with the chores in the horse barn. Depending on the animals' needs, Houston figured he might be able to take the time for breakfast in a couple of hours—or he might not.

With his first sip of the sludge Lloyd passed off as java, Houston remembered the nightmares again. Just last week he'd begun to believe that the haunting images he saw when he closed his eyes were slowly receding. No such luck. Last night, interspersed with intense dreams of Carley, they came back with a vengeance.

Houston supposed that's what he deserved for going to bed with the beautiful and enigmatic Carley on his mind. He'd tried to sort through his impressions of her—without totally giving up on the rest of his life.

Yeah, right.

Like last night when he couldn't eat. And today when he'd have trouble concentrating at work. He sighed and resigned himself to a long, tiring day.

"What in God's name is that horrible noise?" Carley's voice preceded her through the kitchen doorway.

Houston spun around to see the woman who'd been occupying his mind coming toward him in a fury. "Ma'am?"

"Oh, no. We're not going through that ma'am thing again." She smiled and pulled on his shirt-sleeve. "It's Carley, and if you can't hear that dreadful noise you must be deaf. Come with me."

He allowed her to tug him toward the outside door, but only because he was enchanted by the woman. She had on a terry cloth robe, pulled tight in the middle by a nonmatching drawstring. On her dainty feet were two of the rattiest-looking fuzzy slippers in existence.

Her hair... Ah, her hair was the best part of the picture. Sleep tousled and standing straight up in spots, Carley's shoulder-length, auburn tresses formed a cloud of seductive curls around her face. Houston's fingers itched with the need to touch her—any-where—everywhere.

When she pushed at the screen door, his mind cleared enough to question the wisdom of allowing a woman in night clothes to step outside into the darkness. "Uh. Just where are we headed at this hour, little lady?" He held back, pulling against her force.

Carley turned to him and tugged on his sleeve once more. "Outside. Just under my window. I want you to tell me what the noise is that woke me up."

Houston relaxed enough so she could pass through the door and drag him along with her. As they walked around the house's foundation, he marveled at what a vibrant life force this woman named Carley really was. Something had distressed her and disturbed her sleep. Instead of hiding from it, however, here she was, outside the protection of the house, headed straight for the trouble. Fantastic.

They turned a corner, and she came to an abrupt halt. Houston still held the mug and some of the hot coffee sloshed over. Fortunately, it missed his hand.

"There. That's the sound. What is that noise?"

He had to concentrate for a minute. He didn't hear a thing except for the usual night sounds of tree frogs chirping, nighthawk wings whooshing on the wind and various birds calling to their mates in predawn confusion.

"Sorry, Carley, I don't hear anything unusual."

"That shrieking? You don't hear that? It sounds like someone's being attacked."

He tried to sort through the sounds. "You mean the grackles cawing?"

"No. I know what those pesky blackbirds sound like. We had some in the trees outside our apartment. What I'm curious about is that other noise. Like a scream."

Finally it occurred to him that she'd probably never heard that particular sound before.

"Oh, the *chachalacas*." He chuckled and took a sip from his mug. "They're just birds. A little bigger than the grackles and a whole lot noisier, but still, only birds. Did they frighten you?"

"No, they didn't frighten me. I was terrified. That's a bird call?"

"Yep. I'll take you down to the *resaca* sometime. That's where they nest. Interesting-looking birds. They can't fly but they have huge, iridescent green tails."

"Resaca? Chachalaca? I speak some Spanish, but I have no idea what you're talking about."

He gently pulled his forearm from her grip and laid a hand on her shoulder. "Come on. I'll explain it all another time. Right now let's get you back to the house. That's enough big game bird-watching for one morning."

The stars spread enough light over the range for Houston to see Carley's face flush. "Is it morning already? I didn't get much sleep last night."

He thought of his own tossing and turning and felt a kinship he didn't think he was ready to discuss. "Sorry. Bad dreams?"

"No. New place. Strange noises. There are so many strange sounds. And then when I heard the shrieking… Well, I guess I'd been still long enough. I simply had to know what that particular sound was."

Carley opened the screen door, stepped up onto the threshold and turned to face him. He hadn't expected the sudden change of direction and bumped right into her. He reached his one free hand up to steady her and immediately wished he hadn't.

The last bit of coffee in his cup spilled out on the ground. The heat of the night penetrated the still air, and the earth stopped rotating as they gazed into each other's eyes. Like the parched ground of the pastures, the need to drink her in rose up in him.

He slid his hand from her shoulder to her flush-stained neck and let his fingers glide over that silky flesh. "What's happening between us, Carley? Why do I feel as though we're meant to be together?"

The brashness of his remark threw him for a loop. How could he say such things to a near stranger?

But Carley didn't look thrown—or upset. She also didn't answer him. She just looked wide-eyed, soft and sexy as all hell. He took a breath and thought he smelled strawberries again. He figured it shouldn't, but the fragrance turned him on instantly.

Houston's fingers stroked the outline of her jaw. He knew this was crazy, but...he couldn't seem to stop.

Carley exhaled quietly and closed her eyes. He really couldn't help himself. His thumb needed...had to...stroke her full lower lip. Brushing it lightly, he closed his own eyes against the strong sensation. He wanted her desperately.

He felt her eyes pop open at that instant, and he knew she was drawing away, even before she moved. She had a lot more sense than he had.

She turned into the kitchen.

He cleared his throat and tried to sound unaffected. "If I hadn't been here, would you have gone outside? By yourself, I mean."

"Of course, for all the good it would have done me." She laughed softly and put a hand to her hair as if trying to pat down the tangles. "I must look a sight. What are you doing up at this hour, anyway?"

Houston walked to the counter to set down his mug. "I'm always up by now," he said without facing her, trying to steady his badly shaken libido. "Time to start my workday."

When he turned around to finish explaining about ranch chores, he felt a vague wave of nausea—then a thump in the vicinity of his chest. Carley stood in the doorway, leaning one hand against the door frame and smiling at him. Her hair billowed around her head like a burnished cloud. Soft, touchable…and memorable.

A fleeting strand of memory floated in—and back out—of his conscious mind. It was almost like a path to the past had opened in his brain. But as quickly as it came, it was gone.

Houston felt so frustrated at not being able to capture the memory he was speechless. His hands fisted with the anger surging inside him. Why couldn't he simply open the window in his mind and remember?

"Were you about to say something else?" Carley was looking at him as if her entire life depended on whatever he had to say.

The earnestness with which she scrutinized his face softened the anger and dissipated his disappointment. Those strong emotions were quickly replaced with an even stronger desire to drag this woman to his chest and taste the passionate fervor he knew awaited him in her kiss.

He shook his head to bring himself around to the real world before he let emotions rule his actions. "No. I have to go to work. I'll see you later."

Carley felt disconcerted as Houston turned and, without another word, strode out the screen door and into the muted streaks of approaching daylight. She could have sworn she'd seen a faint glimmer of recognition in his eyes a moment ago.

This whole thing was too hard. Not being able to take him in her arms and comfort him when he looked so lost left her emotionally drained. And each time he walked away, her instincts demanded she not let him go—that she keep him within sight at all times.

Carley mounted the stairs toward her room. Time to get Cami up and dressed for the start of another day. As Carley climbed, she couldn't stave off the disappointment dragging her down.

A few days ago Carley had believed she'd been through a life-shattering event when Witt had disappeared. She was wrong. Being close to him without him having his memory back was turning out to be much more difficult. As a matter of fact, it was fast becoming the hardest thing she'd ever done in her life.

Carley's day raced ahead without her complete permission. She would've loved to go out on the ranch, find Houston working, and just follow him around until he looked at her through Witt Davidson's eyes. Or maybe she would curl up in a dark room somewhere and simply wallow in self-pity.

Instead, Cami needed a bath and breakfast. And Carley needed to do some work.

After breakfast mother and daughter inspected the toddlers' playroom, met the three other children Cami's age who would share the morning with her and checked out the competent woman who baby-sat for the youngsters. Carley was a tad concerned about how Cami would take to staying in a strange place all day without her, but she needn't have been. The last sight Carley had of her daughter was when she tried to give her a kiss, only to have Cami ignore her in favor of stealing a block belonging to another little girl.

Carley set out to look around the offices and sleeping rooms that comprised the main house. For an institution, the place didn't feel a bit sterile. The infants and toddlers' rooms were on the first floor of this building. Two nurses shared living quarters with the little ones, and all their rooms were painted in bright, cheery colors. Carley was pleased to find that the rooms didn't smell like disinfectant. They did smell clean, but the overpowering scent was of baby powder.

She also learned that during the day local community volunteers filled in as caretakers for the very youngest. As part of their regular chores, the teenagers living at the home also helped out with the babies after school and on weekends. This week two infants along with the three toddlers were in temporary residence.

Sooner than she would have liked, the time came to behave like an undercover FBI agent. Reid wanted her to dig into the home's files to look for any discrepancies.

Sitting in her new office, and trying her best to concentrate, Carley found herself daydreaming about Houston instead of sorting through the stacks of unfiled paperwork. All the investigations she'd done while Witt had been gone helped her to understand that he'd had some demons in his past. She now knew something of his long-term, unsolved traumas, and that they could have prolonged his actual acceptance of their love. But those childhood problems would not have stood in their way forever. She knew she possessed the training and the love to help him overcome his past and come to terms with himself and with her. Given enough time.

But there hadn't been enough time. Not for her—and not for them.

It took a few minutes for her to swallow back the useless self-analysis and tears. She'd done enough of this kind of retrospection in the past eighteen months to last a lifetime. And she'd rather spend the rest of her time on earth being with the man she loved—even if it meant never retrieving his old personality, memories and love.

The sound of her door squeaking pulled her back into reality. She looked up from her desk to find Doc Luisa standing in her doorway.

"What're you doing, girl?" Doc demanded.

"Huh?" Hey, brilliant response, Dr. Mills. "Uh, I mean, I'm working. Or trying to."

"I thought the definition of a psychologist was one who practiced the science of the mind and mental states...on human beings. Isn't it a little hard to do that buried behind all those files?"

Carley felt herself blush. "Absolutely. But the trouble is that the State expects the kids' records to be kept up to date. The money to help the children can be cut off if the paperwork gets fouled up."

Besides, she thought, Operation Rock-a-Bye could use a break in their investigation.

"Your predecessor didn't pay much attention to the paperwork. He said the woman from the state's Child Protective Services never showed up much, anyway. She sent an assistant around from time to time, but nobody dug into the files or seemed to care a lot about them."

Carley smiled, but wasn't feeling terribly happy. "The files look like everybody has 'dug' into them. They're a mess."

Doc Luisa narrowed her gaze and scrutinized Carley. "A couple of the teenage boys got into a fight last night after dinner. Gabe can't get either one of them to fess up to the problem." Doc fisted her hands on her hips. "Maybe you'd be willing to give it a shot and talk to them?"

Willing? This kind of thing was right up Carley's alley. It seemed like she'd trained all her life for just such a circumstance.

The paperwork would still be here later. "I don't know my way around yet, Doc." Carley pushed away from her desk and stood. "Will you show me where the boys are?"

A couple of hours later one of the boys was leading Carley back to the main house through the maze of barns. She'd gone to talk to him as he'd finished his midmorning chores. And that was exactly what she would have prescribed for him if she'd been able to talk to him beforehand.

Both boys were products of broken homes, and the anger at their circumstances raged just beneath the surface. There hadn't been a "reason" for last night's altercation. They'd just needed to beat out their frustrations.

Hard work was the best thing for both of them. That and the anger-management classes Carley hoped to begin this week.

As they rounded the corner of the barn nearest the house, she heard a high-pitched giggle. A few more feet and Carley saw Houston talking to Rosie, the teenage girl who was so good with Cami.

Both of them tried to wipe guilty looks off their faces as Carley and the boy came near. Carley was deeply curious.

"What's up? Can you share the joke with us?" she asked.

Houston threw a quick glance over his shoulder to

see if anyone was listening, making Carley's curiosity double.

"Shh. Not so loud," he whispered.

Houston Smith had a lot of nerve to shush her, Carley thought. He'd better come to the point in a hurry.

Houston threw his arm around her shoulder and whispered in a conspiratorial tone. "The church council overseeing this place would never approve, so we tend to keep this quiet. A couple of the other counselors and I have been taking the kids for dancing lessons on the weekends. There's a school dance coming up next week, and we thought they should be able to go and not make fools of themselves."

Carley was stunned. "You've been teaching the teenagers to dance? You?"

Houston reared back and looked confused. "Well, yeah. One of the women gave me a few pointers on country-western, but I'm not a half-bad teacher." He removed his arm from Carley's shoulder and narrowed his eyes. "Don't tell me you think the kids shouldn't dance, either...or is it something about me that makes you think I wouldn't know how?"

Think fast, Carley, old girl.

"No. No. I'm sure you're a fine teacher, and the kids should be allowed to participate in the same things as their classmates. It's just—" Carley swallowed hard and let her brain spin into over-drive "—I'd like to help with the teaching, but I don't know the two-step. Do you think maybe you could teach me?"

"I guess so."

"Funny you know the name of the most popular

dance when you claim you don't know how,'' Rosie chimed in.

Carley and Houston both ignored her.

"When?" Carley asked Houston.

"Excuse me?"

She tried to keep the desperation out of her question, but the building need for him made her voice an octave higher anyway. "When can you teach me?"

"Some evening, I suppose."

"How about tonight? I'll even spring for a steak dinner before the lesson."

"I'll need to check with Gabe. See if he wants me to do anything around here tonight. But I imagine it'll be okay."

Carley was thrilled. What could be better than to go dancing with the man you love? He'd have to put his arms around her tonight. "I'll check with Gabe without telling him where we're going exactly. Don't worry. I'm sure it'll be fine," she drawled.

The early afternoon went by quickly for Carley. Lunch, which everyone called dinner, turned into a bigger deal than last night's supper. Turkey, enchiladas, salads, vegetables and a choice of either corn or flour tortillas loaded the table. Carley helped in the kitchen, but spent most of her time watching Lloyd roll the flour tortillas out with the broken end of a broomstick.

After the kids ate, Carley collected Cami and took her on a stroll around the main building. Cami, just learning to walk, seemed to think teetering away from her mother was the best game of the day. After both Mills women were exhausted, Carley managed to put

Cami down for a nap and began preparations for her fantasy night out.

Just as she stepped into the bath, her satellite phone jangled to life, abruptly dragging her back to reality. Thoughts of her boss and real job suddenly landed her feet unsteadily down again on the shifting ground of lost memories and unsolved mysteries.

She flipped open the phone with more force than necessary. "Has anyone ever mentioned that you have an extremely annoying trait of incredibly bad timing, Reid?"

Five

————

"**I**'ll have Manny bring the files out to the ranch late this afternoon," Reid promised from the Houston office. "But you'll find neither the doctor nor the preacher have anything to hide."

Carley's instincts told her that both of them were exactly as they appeared, but she had to follow procedure. "I'll read the reports when I get them. Oh, by the way, tell Manny to get here well before dark, will you? Houston Smith and I have a date for dinner and dancing tonight."

"A date? With the father of your child?"

"He doesn't remember that fact, Reid, and you know it. We're starting over again. Taking things slow."

"Well, good luck, Carley. If any woman on earth could make a man fall in love with her for the second time, it would be you."

"I sure hope you're right." Carley breathed deeply. For everyone's sake, Reid. You just have to be right.

Since Reid had dragged her back to reality and away from a shower, Carley decided to plow through some of the unfinished paperwork on her desk. The afternoon wore on heavily as she tried her best not to think of Houston and their date. This morning had been difficult enough. Just one sight of him and her body betrayed her.

When he touched her she could close her eyes and taste the richness that was all him. She could bring back the images of his probing tongue, heating her and seeking her life's very core.

It was all she could do, when he'd said he felt they somehow belonged together, not to throw her arms around his neck and tell him everything that was in her heart. But the doctor warned her against such a jolt, so she'd sucked up her courage and backed away from him. She wasn't sure she could be so strong again.

Dragging her concentration back to her desk, she found that little pieces of information were missing from nearly every file. That Dan person she'd replaced must have hated to fill in the necessary blanks.

The longer she worked, the worse the situation became. Things were more than a mess. Carley wondered if the state of Texas realized how lax the filing system at this place really was. Not one set of papers on the infants and toddlers seemed to be complete.

Eventually, Carley gave up and placed a call to the nearest office of the Texas Department of Child Protective Services, Licensing Division, looking for the woman supervisor Doc Luisa had mentioned. She reached a Ms. Fabrizio, who spoke with the clipped and efficient manner of a transplanted North-Easterner.

Carley introduced herself and explained her dilemma. "So, how often do you inspect these records?"

"Oh, I never *personally* make inspections. One of my field workers takes care of that."

The woman sounded as if actually having to see a real child might just dirty her hands, Carley thought contemptuously.

"The law in Texas is quite clear, Dr. Mills. We must make on-site inspections every ten to twelve months. In my district we try to inspect facilities twice a year, and each child that is out-placed must have appropriate records with them for transport."

"Do you keep duplicate records?" Carley probed.

"Yes, certainly."

"We don't seem to have all the papers we need in the files. When is your field worker's next inspection?"

"We're due at the ranch in the next ten days. And I would expect all the records to be complete and in proper order when my field worker arrives." The supervisor's voice became high-pitched and tense.

"May I come to your office one day this week, then?" Carley quietly asked. "I need copies of whatever we're missing."

"That's highly irregular. It's not our responsibility to help the foster homes duplicate their state forms."

Carley had heard nasty rumors that some of the bureaucrats on the *other* side of the border insisted on money or favors to do their jobs, but she'd always thought the ones on *this* side were honest and hard-working.

Maybe this particular bureaucrat wanted to be coaxed. "You sound like a reasonable woman," she began. "I'm new to the valley. Would you, by any chance, like to have lunch with me some time this week? Perhaps you can give me a few hints on how to get along while I'm here?"

"Well…"

"Please, Ms. Fabrizio. You name the day and place…be my guest."

No longer reticent, the woman jumped at a chance for a free lunch. She quickly named her day and what Carley felt sure was the most expensive restaurant in the whole valley.

Carley hung up, feeling slimy. She wondered how much each of the copies were going to end up costing her. Ms. Fabrizio was an unknown quantity, and she made Carley nervous.

Rubbing her upper arms as if this warm spring day had suddenly turned cold, Carley tried to put the whole sordid mess out of her mind. She wouldn't have to face the problem again for a few days, and right now she barely had time to take her shower and dress for her night of dancing.

That presented another problem. What did one wear to a country-western dance? A dress? Slacks? Maybe all things named Western called for jeans.

She finally decided dresses were always appropriate for any occasion that involved dancing. Once her mind was made up, Carley closed her files and bounded up the stairs to change. She could barely control her excitement. Dancing was a great excuse to feel Houston's arms around her once more.

The next hour proved more frazzling than exciting. Cami, after rejecting an afternoon nap, whined and fussed, refusing to eat. Carley found a rip in the Western-style dress she intended to wear, and with her hair still damp, the hair dryer caught on fire.

Worse yet, Manny Sanchez arrived when Carley was still in the shower and refused to leave the folders with anyone else but her. Tomorrow she'd have to search him out and retrieve the papers she needed.

By the time Carley dashed into the kitchen, a few minutes late for her date with Houston, she wondered if maybe they'd be better off to skip the whole thing for tonight. Perhaps she could talk him into postponing until tomorrow.

If only Houston…

She halted just inside the doorway and looked up to find him standing next to the screen door talking to Doc Luisa. Carley swallowed the hard lump in her throat that had stopped her cold.

If only Houston…wasn't so dammed gorgeous.

Bareheaded, with his blond hair still wet from his shower, he wore a soft denim shirt that clung to his muscles. When she could drag her gaze away from his chest, she lowered her line of sight and took in well-washed jeans fitting him like a second skin. His contours, the lean waist and wide shoulders, reminded her of their many nights spent exploring each other's bodies—of the sensual zeal and tender ardor that marked his lovemaking.

Both Houston and Luisa turned to look at her. For a second she couldn't move. Then she remembered to breathe. "Sorry I'm late."

Carley wondered what she looked like in their eyes. Her insides were sizzling like a pan filled with hot grease, and her skin stung as if on fire. She adjusted her dress and ran her sweaty palms down her sides.

God help anyone who might even suggest a postponement for tonight.

Doc Luisa angled her head to inspect Carley. "You two going off somewhere this evening?"

Houston opened his mouth to answer, but Carley beat him to it.

"We have a date for dinner and a dancing lesson," she whispered and looked over her shoulder. "You don't mind about the dancing do you? I know Gabe doesn't want..."

"Miz Mills?" Rosie appeared in the doorway holding Cami. "Can you come put Cami to bed? She just kicks and cries when I try to get her into the crib."

Carley headed toward the door. "I'll be back in a few minutes, Houston. Wait for me." She grabbed up Cami and disappeared with Rosie trailing behind.

Houston stood transfixed by the sensations and emotions that Carley stirred inside him. When he finally remembered to close his mouth and turn back to Doc Luisa, he verged on the grim side of anger.

"We do *not* have a date. I only volunteered to teach her the two-step." He tried to soften his tone. None of this was Luisa's fault. "You know I don't date, Doc. I just can't. What if I have a wife or a fiancée somewhere? As long as I can't remember, I won't take the chance of becoming low-down scum."

Luisa laid her hand on his forearm, forcing Houston to gaze into her eyes. He saw a different kind of look in the woman's eyes tonight. Kinder, softer, warmer.

Ever since he'd woken up in her spare bedroom all those months ago, Luisa's eyes became wary when she studied him—as if she needed to hold back some part of her emotions. But tonight all that edginess was gone.

"You *do* feel something for Carley. I can see it plainly written on your face when you look at her. Why don't you give her a chance, son?"

"But..." He pulled his arm free and drove his fingers through his hair.

"Look," Luisa began. "The woman is a psychologist, isn't she? Why don't you tell her about losing your memory? Maybe she can help. At the very least, I'll bet she's a good listener."

"Well...if you think we can trust her, maybe it wouldn't hurt to get her opinion."

"Oh, I'm sure you can trust her. I can tell she has a good heart...that she'd never do anything to hurt you. Give it a try. What have you got to lose?"

Houston didn't know if Carley had a good heart, but she sure had one terrific body.

They rode in silence on the way to the Wrangler Café on the outskirts of McAllen. He'd picked the place because he knew they would get a decent meal, and the band could play a mean two-step. They arrived early, and he held the door open for her. The minute they stepped inside the poorly lit bar, the few ranch hands that were there quit eating and turned to stare.

Of course, Houston had to admit Carley was worth a gape or two. Tonight she positively glowed. She wore a bright-red dress—shiny and tight. Tight enough to show every curve. And she sure had an abundance of those.

The dress dipped in front to a vee, ending in the valley between her full breasts. That dang dress also ended way above her knees, exposing impossibly long legs. So much of her skin showed he didn't know where to look first. So he tried to sneak a peek everywhere at once.

At least, he'd thought he wanted to take it all in, until the cowpokes at the bar whistled approvingly at Carley. She made a dramatic curtsy and grinned at the boys. Meanwhile, Houston pulled her into a shadowy corner. If he'd thought he could leave Carley alone for one minute, he would run out to the truck and get the horse blanket from the back to cover her up.

"Whatever possessed you to wear that getup?" he growled when he'd seated them both at a table.

Her bright smile dimmed, and he felt as if he'd deliberately blocked out the sun. What was it about this woman that made him totally lose his mind, anyway?

"I thought you'd like it. I wasn't sure what to wear for dancing the two-step," she said a little sadly.

"I do like it." He wanted to say something to make her smile again. "You look beautiful. Too beautiful for a place like this."

That was no polite lie. *Beautiful* hardly covered the way she looked tonight. Even in this unilluminated corner, her mahogany hair shone with burnished lights. Her skin looked soft—touchable and silky. And when she smiled at his comment, her face glowed with a healthy beauty. Houston didn't think Carley wore any makeup this evening, or needed any for that matter.

The longer he gazed at her, the more he felt mesmerized by her eyes. Suddenly snapping back to reality, Houston caught his hand in midair right before he touched her face. His fingers longed to trace the outline of her jaw, to linger against that creamy surface.

He jerked his hand away, shook his head and cleared his throat. This wasn't the way he'd imagined the evening would go.

The waitress showed up with an order pad in hand. "What'll you have?"

Carley looked confused. "We haven't seen a menu yet."

"We don't have menus. What'll you have?"

Now Carley looked annoyed. "What do you serve?"

The waitress rolled her eyes and shifted all her weight to one foot. "Look, lady, this is a steak place. We've got rib-eyes, twenty-ounce sirloins, fillet mignon and, if your taste buds run hot, steak-fajita tacos…but they're all steak. Now, how do you want your steak cooked?"

Carley raised an obviously irritated eyebrow at the surly young woman. "I'll have a fillet, cooked medium, with a baked potato and salad with blue cheese dressing." She gestured to Houston. "He'll have the sirloin, bloody, with fries and refried beans. And bring us both a long-neck beer…put mine in a glass, please."

"Why didn't you just say so?" The waitress twirled around and headed for the bar.

Houston's surprise at that whole scene made him shake his head in wonder. "Carley, you just ordered for me."

She jerked around to face him. "Uh…yeah. Do you mind? I'm so used to ordering for Cami that I guess it's become a bad habit. I didn't mean to be so pushy.''

"That's not the point. How'd you know what I wanted?''

"Did you want something else?''

"No. You ordered exactly what I'd decided to have.'' Houston's surprise turned into skepticism. "You took the words right out of my mouth. That's pretty good…guessing. Or do you also read minds?''

Carley's mouth cracked into a sheepish grin. "I'm a psychologist, remember? I've, um, made a study of people's tastes. You just look like a man who'd want his steak rare.''

"Yeah, I suppose so.'' For a second Houston saw a flash of some old scene in his brain. But the image vanished before he could capture the memory.

Carley had just reminded him of why he'd agreed to come tonight. "I'd like to talk to you about something. Patient to psychologist, so to speak. If you wouldn't mind?''

She stared silently into his eyes for a minute too long. What did she see when she looked at him that way?

"Of course not. What can I do for you?''

"I…'' He glanced around one more time to be certain no one sat within earshot. "I don't know who I am.''

Staring at her hands, she swallowed hard, thought a minute, and when she finally looked up at him, her eyes danced with amusement. "Do you mean literally, or existentially?''

"This isn't funny. If you're going to make a joke, forget I said anything.''

Carley laid her hand on top of his, and zinging heat

singed him. "I'm sorry. Please continue." Her sugar-coated voice wrapped around him like a soft, warm coat on a winter day.

Houston silently swore he'd heard that tone in her voice before...somehow. But he couldn't breathe while she continued to touch him.

"I woke up a year and a half ago with no memory." He pulled his hand free. "It's like a nightmare I can't shake."

"That...must be terrible." The look in her eyes turned to hurt, as if she could feel his pain. "Don't you remember anything at all?"

Houston wished he hadn't started this. He didn't want her to go through any of the agony that he'd felt, and she seemed so sensitive to him. "I have what I call 'dreams.' But they're more like still photographs...or flash cards. They kinda float through my mind...watery and indistinct."

"Would you say they're like little islands of memory?"

"Sort of. Except these islands are under the water. All blurry and fuzzy."

"Hmm. Why don't you tell me whatever you can about these images? Do any of them stick with you?"

"Some. I think I've lived on a ranch or farm at some time. I remember working with animals."

"Well, that's something. Anything else? Do you remember any people or faces?"

Houston closed his eyes and tried to concentrate, but a stabbing pain blindsided him. He hadn't been expecting the lightning jolt to his temple. His eyes popped open and he rubbed at the side of his head. "There's something...something close to the surface.

I think it's a woman's face, but…no, never mind. It's gone again.''

Carley blew out a huge breath, as if she'd been holding it for a long time. ''Can you remember anything about the woman? Color of eyes…outstanding features?''

''No, not really. There's blackness around her, and pain. I can feel the pain.'' He absentmindedly touched his temple once more.

The waitress arrived with their beers. ''Food'll be out in a minute, folks,'' she announced, turning to another table.

Carley smiled and poured her beer into the icy glass. ''Don't force anything. And don't do anything that hurts. That could make it worse.'' She took a sip, and the tip of her tongue languidly licked the foam from around her upper lip.

Houston could do nothing but stare at Carley's mouth. The sight of her slowly licking away the bubbles was erotic as hell. His mind immediately pictured her tongue licking his lips, his tongue, his skin, his…

He took a big sip from the bottle, then placed the cold glass against his forehead. When he had his body back under control, he opened his eyes to find her scrutinizing him.

''What?''

''I just wondered how you picked the name Houston. Did someone help you?''

''Oh, that.'' He chuckled and swallowed another swig of beer. ''I was shot and beat up pretty badly. Wasn't found with a wallet or ID, and my clothes were in tatters. Doc Luisa patched me back to health. When she looked for hints about my identity, she noticed a label from a department store in Houston in my ripped pants. The name of the city kinda rang a bell, and seemed like the only thing that really meant something. I just took it for my own.''

The skinny young waitress showed up with huge platters of food layered across her arms. Houston was grateful for the reprieve from talking about himself. Plus, the tantalizing smells of steak grilling had left him starving.

As desolate as Carley felt, she wouldn't let her misery show. Obviously, the man tried his best to remember. The memories of his past life...of her...were locked inside his brain behind a door he just couldn't force open. In silence she picked at her food.

After the plates were cleared away, she took a beginner's two-step lesson from him. The two-step came easily enough after all her years of calisthenics and ballroom dancing lessons. But the two-step wasn't what she'd really wanted. The dance turned out to be fun and lively, but it wasn't close. Carley desperately wanted to be *close*.

In a little while the band began the strains of an old, half-forgotten standard, redone in slow, country-style. Houston stood in the middle of the dance floor for a moment and narrowed his eyes at her in some unspoken question.

When he reached for her hand, she gave him hers slowly, tentatively. The look in his eyes stumped her, but she tried to act casual and unconcerned. What did he expect from her? She would give him the world. But he had to ask. She wasn't allowed to tell him.

Houston drew her into his arms. Carley put one hand on his shoulder while he continued to hold her fingers in his own. He slid his right arm around her waist and placed the palm of his hand flat in the small of her back.

She closed her eyes and inhaled the spicy scent of aftershave and beer, mixed together with a hint of a musky smell she remembered so clearly—the smell that haunted her dreams.

Carley inched closer to his warmth and nuzzled into the vee in his neck, under his chin, where she'd always fitted so well. Nothing had changed. Nothing but the fact that this was Houston Smith—not her lost lover, Witt Davidson.

He pulled her closer still and edged his leg between hers to guide their movements. They moved around the border of the darkened dance floor, but within seconds Carley was lost. Lost in the music. Lost in her dreams.

She could feel the wisps of chest hair that escaped the top button of his shirt as they tickled her cheek. She could feel the beating of his heart in time with hers. Right here was where she'd longed to be. In his arms was where she wanted to stay.

A few of the lyrics seeped inside her head. Something about "the memory of a love's refrain...dreaming in vain...haunting...reverie." The heat in the room became oppressive, and the ache in her chest grew stronger.

Houston brought their clasped hands into his chest and lowered his head so that his lips were next to her ear. Carley heard him breathing, hot and heavy. A trickle of sweat formed at her temple.

When he ringed her earlobe with his tongue, Carley heard herself make a little sound that reminded her of a strangled gasp. But instead of slowing him down, it seemed only to encourage him. As her body loosened, his tightened. As she fitted more snugly against him, his muscles bunched and flexed.

Houston gently sucked her earlobe into his mouth and tugged. The pull rocketed down her body, stopping to peak her breasts, then moved lower to pool between her legs with enough heat and wetness to make her squirm.

The two dancers melded together, as close as the thin layers of clothes would allow. So close that Carley felt his arousal pressing into the flesh of her belly.

Houston let go of her earlobe and placed tiny kisses along her jawline. As he drew nearer to her mouth, she turned into the kiss. His lips were sweet, warm and gentle—barely a whisper against hers.

She wanted him closer still. Wanted the feel of his skin gliding along hers. Carley couldn't hold back another moan.

He answered her moan with a murmur against her lips. ''Charleston, darlin'.''

Carley's heart did a little flip. She loved it when Witt used her given name. So few people ever called her by the name her father had bestowed on her before he died.

Suddenly her eyes flew open. *Witt? Charleston?* She used the palms of her hands to push on his chest. Carley leaned her head back and looked at the man whose arms were still tight around her.

''What did you just call me?''

Houston's eyes were glazed, unfocused. ''What? I don't know.''

''You called me Charleston. How did you know that's my real name?''

He licked his lips and shook his head slightly. "I guess I must have heard someone call you that."

"No, Houston. No, you haven't. I've never been anything but Carley around you." She turned her head to find the music stopped and the rest of the dance floor empty.

She took a step back from him and studied his face as he tried to come out of his sexual trance and concentrate on what just happened between them. Carley felt cold and wrapped her arms around her waist to hold herself steady.

Houston swiped a hand across his face. When his eyes opened again, they were steel grey and sharp. "We've done that before, haven't we? Danced, kissed...been together?"

"Yes. Are you all right?"

"Why? Why didn't you tell me?" His eyes narrowed into slits. "What were we to each other? Were we married?"

She remained silent but shook her head.

"Lovers, then?"

"Yes, but..."

He held up his hand, palm out, to stop her speech. "You let me rattle on about losing my memory and said nothing? You just let me think I was kissing a stranger when all the while..."

Houston clamped his mouth shut and gingerly rubbed his left temple. "I can't deal with this right now," he finally managed. He spun himself around, heading straight past tables full of diners and directly toward the front door to the parking lot.

Carley nearly panicked. He couldn't be mad at her. So much was at stake. She simply had to make them allies—had to make him trust her.

She dashed past the staring strangers and dragged open the heavy nightclub door. Stepping into the calm but humid evening, she tried to adjust the focus of her eyes. Through the starlit parking lot, she saw Houston slam the driver's door of the huge pickup. The engine grumbled to life.

Oh, God, no!

Her heart thudded against her ribs, and her knees turned to jelly, making her feel as if she was moving in slow motion. Flashes of jumbled thoughts exploded in her head as she tried to run across the parking lot in her spiky high heels.

She had to make him listen to her. But what could she say? She couldn't just blurt out the whole truth and tell him who he was and that she loved him. What if that forced his memories to disappear forever?

Carley wanted her man back in one piece—whole and capable of returning to the operation. Otherwise Reid would put him in protective custody. He'd end up in an institution.

This just couldn't be happening. There was danger for him at every turn. She had to do something…say something. She had to stop him from running, and calm him down.

Out of breath, she finally reached the truck as it thundered noisily in place.

"Houston, you don't understand. Wait!"

Six

Houston sat, blankly staring out the windshield of the four-by-four pickup, his white-knuckled fingers wrapped around the steering wheel in a death grip. Blinded by the searing pain in his head and frozen with anger and confusion, he couldn't move enough to put the doggone transmission into gear. Besides, deep inside, a little voice told him that no matter what, it was not in him to leave a woman stranded in a strange place.

His head told him Carley had betrayed him, but his heart…well, he couldn't quite tell what was in his heart when it came to Charleston Mills.

On the dance floor he'd been entranced by her—literally. She'd felt so right in his arms. The lighting, the soft music, her yielding body, all seemed so familiar. Houston knew he'd totally lost control. If she hadn't turned out to be an old flame, he'd be down-right embarrassed by his behavior in a public place.

She'd tricked him. Lied to him. Damn her.

A soft knock on the passenger window roused him from his haze of anger. He reached over and unlocked the door, quickly turning to face forward again. He couldn't look at her face. Carley was so beautiful, so full of life and lust. He'd dreamed about her last night, tossed and turned with wanting her. And all the while, in reality, she'd known him—known him in the most intimate way.

Houston turned the key again, silencing the engine.

All he knew for sure was that Carley was not the same woman from his nightmares. She couldn't be the woman who caused the excruciating terror. There must have been another. Had he hurt someone else so badly that he could feel her pain every time he closed his eyes?

Carley opened the door and slipped into the truck. For one uncomfortable minute, she sat silently staring straight ahead, the same as he did, taking several deep breaths.

Turning to face him, she pleaded, "Please give me a chance to explain. I didn't mean to hurt you. I'm only trying to do what's best...to do the right thing."

Houston spun to face her, but his hands still gripped the wheel. "Lying to me was the 'right' thing?"

"I didn't lie. I...just didn't tell you the truth. Believe me, there is a difference."

He couldn't continue to look at her, but he couldn't force his eyes away, either. "Right. Why don't you explain the difference to me?"

"I'm a psychologist. You do remember that, don't you?"

At his stony silence, she took another deep breath and continued. "When I realized you'd lost your memory, I contacted a specialist in amnesia. He warned me against rushing to tell you about your past. He claimed that if you push yourself to remember, there's a possibility you'll bury the memories so deeply you'll never be able to retrieve them."

Houston gritted his teeth. How could Carley sit there looking so calm? Every fiber inside him was stretched tighter than the rope holding a calf's legs right before its rump felt the branding iron.

"I was prepared to wait until you remembered me before..."

His desperation and need caused him to blurt out, "I'm sorry, but I don't remember you. Not really."

The anguish shone clearly in her eyes. When he saw her tears welling up, all his anger disappeared, leaving utter and complete frustration.

He bent his head to the steering wheel and beat his hand against the dashboard. "Oh, God. Who am I?"

She put a gentle hand on his shoulder, causing more sensations in him than simple comforting should.

"A good man. Brave and strong—and caring," she whispered. "You'll get through this. I'm here to help."

"I don't want your kind of help, dammit!" Houston jerked his shoulder from her light touch.

When Carley gasped and pulled her hand back to her chest in a defensive motion, Houston felt like a real heel. He swallowed back his rising turmoil. "I want to remember you. I want to remember everything, but it's just not happening. Your being here only seems to add to my confusion.''

In the glare of the parking lot lights, he saw her bite down on her lip and stare at him with a pain that matched his own. The tug in his heart surprised him.

''Tell me, what is my name?''

Again, her hurt and haunted look tortured his soul.

''Witt.'' Her voice was rough and filled with pain, and she cleared her throat to go on. ''Witt Davidson.''

''Witt?'' Houston rolled the name across his tongue, tasting the consonants, listening to the sound. ''Not much of a name, is it?''

''I always thought it was a good name…that it was as strong as you are.''

He nearly spit the name back in her face, but held his temper. ''I'd appreciate it if you'd call me Houston.'' He didn't feel the least bit strong. In fact, he noticed his hands were shaking, so he grabbed the wheel again. ''That's the name I can hold on to. The only one I recognize.''

Carley smiled softly. ''Of course. I told you, you're better off not to rush things. If you try too hard, you may bury the truth forever.''

''Do I have a family? Parents? Brothers and sisters…or maybe a…wife and kids who might need me?''

''Your parents died when you were young. Your grandparents raised you on a ranch in West Texas. They're gone now, too. You were an only child and have never been married.''

''So no one cares one way or the other if I'm lost?''

''I care.''

''That brings up another good question. How'd you

find me? And why?'' Suddenly he worried that she might yet turn out to be a threat to his safety.

''Manny Sanchez. You and he worked together once a few years ago. He recognized you and notified me.''

''Manny?'' So it was true. If you couldn't remember your past, you never knew who to trust. ''What…what kind of work? Criminal? Or something legit? And why you?''

''Definitely not criminal.'' She studied him with an intensity that shook him. Carley lowered her voice to a conspiratorial whisper. ''Besides being lovers once, we worked together as partners. You and I are lawmen, Houston. You're one of the good guys. I'm confident you'll eventually remember and be able to go back. You just need time.''

He swung his body around to face her squarely and tightened his jaw. ''Tell me how I was hurt. Who shot me?''

She tore her gaze from him. ''I don't know. I wish I did. You disappeared. You were there…and then suddenly you were gone.'' Her voice shook and she dropped her chin.

The frustration welled up, making him blind with need. He grabbed her shoulders and lasered a kiss across her lips, the lips that were driving him crazier than he already must be. At first she sat stunned, then she moaned slightly under his assault and opened her mouth, beckoning him to take more. Damn her.

Instead of the half-awake, tender kisses he'd given her on the dance floor, Houston poured all his frustration and rage into this kiss. He ravaged her mouth, thrusting his tongue deeply inside and dueling with hers. While his fingers dug into her upper arms, he jammed her chest tightly into his, flattening her breasts against him.

The rough treatment didn't appear to frighten Carley. On the contrary, she gave back as good as she got. She wrapped her arms around his neck and clung to him.

When at last he had to take a breath, he broke away from her with a jolt, gasping for air. Gazing at her heavy-lidded eyes and kiss-swollen lips, he knew he still didn't remember, still was at a loss for a past life.

The fact that she knew more about him than he knew about himself was nearly unbearable. The woman in his arms had a history, and she held the keys to his past, as well.

"I can't…I don't want to hear any more." He pushed her back against the truck's seat, cranked it to life, jammed it into reverse and mashed the gas pedal.

Houston's nightmares came crashing back, causing him to slam on the brakes. Deep in his gut he believed what she'd said. He was a lawman, not the one who'd brought this pain down on himself. Then who? What evil had done this thing to him?

He raked his hand across his forehead and stepped on the gas again. The pickup skidded across the caliche parking lot, throwing dust and tiny rocks in its wake.

"You're going to have to give me more time. I need to digest all this information." He was concentrating on the road in front of him, but could feel Carley's stress as surely as if he witnessed it in her eyes.

"I want to help. Please, Houston, don't shut me out." She reached to touch his arm, but then hesitatingly withdrew her hand. "I won't hurt you, but maybe I could…"

"No." His reply reverberated in the closed cab. He glanced over at her hurt look, and his heart softened as he saw tears welling behind those long lashes once again.

Hell. He didn't want to hurt her. But he had to protect himself. Had to think.

"Look. I'm going to be real busy on the ranch for the next few days. The drought has hit us hard."

He took a breath and calmed his voice. "The cattle are starving because the grass has dried up. They'd be happy to eat the prickly pear cactus, but we can't let them near the stuff. It plays hell with their stomachs." He guided the truck onto the farm road leading to the ranch. "We're going out on the range to try burning the prickles off the cactus. Gives the cattle something to chew. Buys us a little time while we pray for spring rains."

"Can I help?"

"The work is hot and nasty, Carley. Some of the boys and I will camp out on the range, so we'll have more daylight. We'll have to work fast. The cattle are ready to drop." Houston pulled the pickup into the dirt yard of the main house and slammed on the brakes. "There's nothing you can do. I won't even have time to think, and, to be honest, that's just what I need to do right now. Will you still be here when we're done?"

"I'll be here."

"Well, then…maybe we can talk some more later."

Her face glowed with a hopeful expression. His gut told him not to let her set her sights on him going back to being her partner—or her lover. If he never remembered his past, he wouldn't be able to stand knowing she remembered who he'd been before. It would hurt too much.

"Or maybe there'll be nothing much to talk about," he mumbled. "We'll see."

The next morning dawned hot and humid, but Carley barely cared. Her night had been both warm and steamy as she tossed and turned, going over and over Houston's words...the kisses they'd shared.

She'd thought, when he told her he didn't want her around, that her world had stopped spinning. Her heart stuttered, and it was all she could do to make it beat normally once more. He wasn't going to let her help him. He wasn't even going to give her the time for a new start in their relationship. The worst thing of all was that he didn't trust her. Didn't trust her not to hurt him.

Carley went through the early-morning motions of getting Cami up and dressed, but her heart wasn't in it. Cami must have sensed her mother's unhappiness and, not knowing how to help or what was wrong, she did what all babies do when things aren't right. She cried. And whined. And generally made a complete irritant of herself.

"You're being a pill this morning, Cami. Please be good. Mama's on the verge of a good cry as it is. You're not helping things." Carley finally finished tying Cami's shoelace and set her down on the floor. "Want to walk to breakfast on your own two feet? Come on, you can do it."

Cami looked surprised at being upright. She'd been taking steps for weeks now, but she'd always held on to something or someone. The shock of standing alone caused her to find her balance the fastest way she knew how—she plopped smack on her bottom and let out a howl of fury.

Carley sighed and reached to pull Cami upright by her hands. "Nobody trusts me these days, I guess." Once Cami was steady on her feet, Carley let go of one hand, keeping a tight grip on the other. "All right. You can do this by yourself, but you don't believe me yet. We'll go together. I won't let go."

Nothing went right, of course. Cami fussed all through her breakfast. Carley dropped a full cup of coffee over herself and the kitchen floor. Finally, after all the catastrophes had been cleared up, Carley tried to leave Cami in the day room but the baby grabbed at her neck and screamed like she was mortally wounded.

None of the women caretakers or the other children could entice Cami to let go and stay with them. She fisted her hands in Carley's hair and wailed. Carley figured Cami was acting out all the pain and anxiety emanating from her mother, so she simply sat down on the linoleum tile with Cami in her arms and rocked her. Cami buried her head in her mother's shoulder and sobbed.

Pretty soon some of the other toddlers came to comfort their unhappy playmate. They wanted to help make things better for Cami, but they didn't know how any more than Cami knew why she was so unhappy.

One tender-hearted, dark-haired girl placed her hand on Cami's back and patted softly. "*'Ta bueno.* All better," she murmured.

Carley's emotions did a double flip. She'd been

feeling so sorry for herself and her fatherless child that she'd forgotten about these other children who had no one at all to hold them. Yet here they were, trying to comfort Cami in her hour of need.

While she rocked Cami in her lap, Carley studied the toddler who still patted her daughter. The little girl's big brown eyes and dark skin clearly spoke of a Mexican-American heritage. How did this child, or any of the other babies, end up in an out-of-the-way foster home like Casa de Valle?

Curious, and determined to get answers to these children's origins as well as to Reid's questions on the legitimacy of their reasons for being here, Carley decided to make a concerted effort at organizing the files. She set Cami down in the middle of her friends and got to her feet. If these little waifs could be strong, so could Carley, by God.

She straightened her clothes and cleared her throat. "Cami, it's time for me to go to work." The stern tone she used was unmistakable. "You be a good girl and play with your friends. I'll see you later."

Carley walked to the door, heading for her office. When she glanced back, Cami didn't turn around.

A couple of days later Carley phoned Reid and managed to catch him in his office. He sounded rushed and irritated, but he took the time to listen to her problems.

"These files are impossible. I'm beginning to believe someone deliberately mishandled them," she began. "And Houston hasn't showed up since…well, since our date."

"I'm not happy about Davidson being off on his own with no memory of who he is," Reid said.

"The kids in my anger-management class tell me he's safer out with the cows than he is in a car on the Interstate. Apparently, he really knows his way around the open range."

"He'd better be back today. I want you protecting him. Is that clear?"

"Yes, sir." Carley hesitated to make her request, with her boss so obviously harried and overworked, but she needed his help. "Reid, can you get a hold of the state's microfilmed copies of Casa de Valle's placement records?"

"Uh. It might take a while. There are channels to go through, you know. We might even have to get a subpoena."

"Could you at least try? I've been trying to get the help of a local supervisor at Child Protective Services. I'm even taking her to lunch this week. But I'm afraid she'll end up being a stonewall."

"Right. I'll start the paperwork from this end. Maybe I can find one of my old buddies in the state records department to speed up the process. You need anything else?"

"More time. I don't think that a couple of weeks is going to be enough to give it a fair trial with Houston."

"No can do. Ten more days is all I can spare. Things are nearing a head as it is. I need you back here. We've even had to pull Manny out of the valley to do some undercover work in Mexico.

"Oh, by the way, he put your folders in the United States Priority mail. Best way I could think of to guarantee you'd get them delivered into your hands."

"Manny's not here in the Rio Grande Valley anymore?'' She'd been so sure he'd be around if something went wrong.

''No. And you need to keep watching your back. An informant claims a major baby exchange is going to take place sometime in the next ten days. We haven't been able to tie anything directly to your foster home, but I'm having one of my gut feelings about that place. I'm just positive you're sitting close to the heart of this ring.''

''Should I move the children out of harm's way?''

''No. The kids should be fine. Besides, we don't want to spook the bad guys into running for cover. Just keep your eyes open and if you think you need backup, we'll be nearby.''

By the time Carley clicked off her cell phone, the weight of the handset felt ten times heavier than it had a few minutes before. Her heart was heavier, too. She wouldn't have enough time to change Houston's mind and make him trust her. In fact, Carley had the distinct impression that within ten days their time would've totally run out.

Houston wiped the sweat off his brow with his kerchief and replaced his hat. Holding the mare's reins lightly, he'd stopped briefly while leading her through the 4-H barn toward the corral. The last few days had taken their toll on him and the horses.

He and the other men had done what they could for the cattle. A neighboring farm had even brought over a load of hay. Anything else was in the hands of Mother Nature.

Houston was glad for the time to let the horses and men rest for a while. But he needed to find more hard work for himself to do, and in a hurry.

The minute his work stopped, the images returned. Images he'd only dreamed about. Images of Carley lying under him, smiling that seductive way she had, with her arms raised, pleading with him to come to her. Once more his fingers tingled with the phantom feel of her skin, but this time he suspected the memories were real and not merely wishful thinking.

Fortunately, he hadn't seen her in person since the night he'd told her to give him some time. Hah! That was a joke if he ever heard one. Not seeing her in person didn't stop him from seeing her in his dreams, both at night and during the day. Instead of keeping his mind on business, every time he turned around, he smelled strawberries.

He couldn't concentrate on anything. The ranch's paperwork was backing up past the ridiculous point, and the new schedules for the kids still sat on his desk awaiting approval.

Today was the first day of summer vacation for the school-age children living at the foster home, and by tomorrow morning the barn would be full of rowdy preteens waiting for instructions about new chores.

Houston shook off the dreams and headed toward his office in the back of the children's barnyard. He stopped to check on the live 4-H projects as they calmly awaited their charges' attention. Pigs, chickens, calves, sheep—all quietly chewed on special feed.

He should be annoyed by the extra work the kids' projects caused him, but he wasn't. Actually, the baby animals were kinda cute, and the way each of the children pitched in to take care of their charges warmed his heart. It was good to see these cast-off kids give and receive love from the animals. And all the hard work made for strong and healthy bodies.

But he had to hurry and finish the instruction sheets before the first wave of kids hit the barn. He gently pulled the mare's reins and made a quick U-turn from the mangers where he'd been staring down at the animals.

All of a sudden, something hit his shin—hard.

At the same time he looked to see what hit him, a loud squeal came from the object now clinging to his jeans below the knees. It was one of the toddlers from the dayroom. The baby had turned and was about to take off in a path that would lead directly under the horse's hooves.

"Whoa. Hold on there, pint-size. Where you headed all by yourself?" Houston scooped up the child just in time to keep the kid from being trampled. "Whew. You nearly bought the farm, little one."

The toddler was all wiggles and giggles. Houston held on even though the kid was as slippery as one of those calves they greased at the fair. He figured this must be a little girl since she was dressed in pink ruffles, now completely smeared in mud. When she finally quieted some, he used his fingers to rub at the caked mud on her face.

"Well, I'll be…if it isn't Carley's little girl. What was your name, baby? Cami wasn't it?"

The baby looked up at him and her eyes widened. Houston had thought at first that the toddler's eyes were the same color as Carley's. But this close, he could see that they were shaped like Carley's with the color being more along the lines of blue green with a touch of gray. Interesting combination.

Cami's expression was so serious that for a minute

Houston was afraid she'd burst out in tears. He turned his head to search for the adult who must be looking after this child. If she started crying, he had no idea what to do for her. Bad enough that he had to pick up the one kid guaranteed to make him nervous.

Cami placed a grubby little hand against Houston's cheek and got his attention. "Da-da."

Poor little fatherless tyke, he thought. She's so in need of a man in her life that she'll latch on to the first male who holds her.

And hold her he did—tightly to his chest. As he studied her a little closer, he realized how very alike her features were to his own. The longer he held his arms around her the less nervous he became—almost like she belonged right there. Could she be his? Was it possible?

Impossible. Carley would have told him. She wouldn't keep something this important from him.

He remembered her saying, "Besides being lovers once…" That sounded like a long time ago. His memories of the woman in his mind were stronger, fresher. He must have been in a relationship with that woman right before he'd disappeared.

And the way Carley had talked about the baby's father…nope, it just didn't add up. That Cami looked like him and felt so right in his arms was simply a coincidence.

Another sudden, unbidden thought crossed his mind. Why couldn't he be a surrogate father to Carley's daughter while they were here on the ranch? He'd love to have a hand in her raising, to step in where the jerk who'd left her behind should be.

After the last few days of thinking, Houston knew one thing for sure. He needed more time with Carley—desperately needed to find out if she felt what he'd been feeling, or if she could forget the past and forge a future with him.

This needy child was another good reason Houston wanted to renew his relationship with Carley. Maybe if…

"Cami! Oh, thank heaven you're all right." Carley raced into the barn and tugged her daughter from Houston's arms. "She pulled away from Rosie on the way out here."

Carley put a hand on Cami's hair, and Houston sensed she was reassuring herself of the baby's welfare by touching her. But Carley was gazing at him. Every dream he'd had of her for the past few days slammed against him hard enough to knock him down.

A beautiful and sexy woman, Carley was obviously intelligent and a loving mother to her child. His heart beat a little stronger in his chest. He looked at Cami and then into her mother's eyes. A powerful yearning for them both rose from deep inside, making his chest ache. He absently rubbed at the spot, and wondered what in hell the lady had ever seen in him before he'd lost his memory.

A dark and sinister thought struck him right between the eyes while he wasn't looking. If Cami wasn't his, then while he was off with the other woman, Carley had slept with someone else.

She'd claimed to have loved him before he vanished, but it sure looked like someone else had helped her get over the loneliness pretty quick.

Damn.

Seven

"Thanks for catching Cami," Carley gasped, snuggling her daughter closer to her chest. "I was helping the girls bring the toddlers out to see your baby animals."

She gulped for air and nervously laughed at the same time. "My daughter picked a fine time to go from shaky steps to running foot races."

Houston stood close, scrutinizing them with an intensity that made her warm all over. He looked absolutely fabulous today, with sweat beading on his forehead and jeans riding low on his hips. Carley's fingers wriggled with the desire to touch him. Fighting the strong urge, she tightened her grip on Cami to keep her hands still.

He studied her and Cami with those pale-blue eyes, lost behind long, blond lashes. What thoughts did he have about the two of them? Could it be that the door to his memory was easing open?

Raucous squeals signaled that the other toddlers, led by older children and a few adults, were scampering into the barn. Their noisy chattering and little cries of delight broke the quiet stillness of animals chewing their feed.

The toddlers ran toward the various animal pens. A half dozen chubby little arms tried to reach between the bars and touch the now frightened creatures. Each of the children had a caretaker nearby, and they scrambled to keep the kids from harming themselves or the young animals. Tiny specks of hay rose in the air, mingling with the hazy sunlight streaming into the barn. Chaos reigned.

Carley figured, since Cami had been the first to see the animals, that she'd want to be down with the others to pet any young critter within range. But as Carley began to lower Cami back to the ground, she was stopped by her daughter's rapt expression. Cami was more intent on the tall, lanky cowboy than on anything happening around her.

Carley's attention shifted immediately to Houston, and she sensed the man and the child had reached some turning point. Cami grinned her famous, baby-toothed smile at her father. For his part, Houston didn't seem capable of keeping a scowl on his face, either. When Cami reached for him, Houston held out his arms and took the toddler into his embrace.

"Hey, little girl, don't you want to see the babies, too?" Houston crooned.

Cami stared at him for a minute, then wrapped her arms around his neck and hugged him tight.

Carley felt the ache in her heart spreading out to

capture every inch of her body. The longing for this
man to want them both was so strong she nearly wept.
But Carley merely sniffed once, then kept herself still.
Houston had said he didn't want her help. For them
to ever have a chance at becoming a family, he would
have to trust her. He would have to ask about Cami.
Carley couldn't just blurt it out.

Carley could see Houston's attention was totally
captured by the toddler in his arms. Perhaps Cami
would be the key to unlocking the doors in his mind.

Cami reared back to gaze at Houston's face. Then
her typical one-year-old attention span wavered. She
caught sight of the saddled horse that Houston had
been about to lead through the 4-H barn, and her eyes
lit up.

"Mine!"

Houston turned to look at his horse, but quickly
turned back to Carley. "What's she saying?"

Carley felt her lips curl up at the corners. "She
wants the horse. Maybe you could let her pet him?"

Houston's face creased with a huge grin, matching
his daughter's smile exactly. "Smart kid. The mare's
a female not a male, though, and she's one of the
gentlest, most easygoing horses in the state." He
moved toward the horse, keeping a tight hold on
Cami. "I don't blame you for wanting her and not
the other critters, Cami. The mare's smarter, and
she'll hold still while you touch her."

Cami leaned so far out of Houston's arms to reach
for the horse that Carley feared her daughter would
tear herself from his grip. But Houston adjusted his
hands and grabbed her under the arms so she couldn't
squirm and fall. He held Cami like the precious cargo
she was, and Carley had to swallow back her emo-

tions. The sight of the man and child together seemed so right.

When Cami had a huge handful of the horse's mane, Houston turned back to Carley. "She's got a good grip. I'll bet she'll make a great horsewoman. Think it would be all right if I let her sit in the saddle?"

"Well…" Before Carley could voice her concerns about putting a baby on such an intimidating animal, Houston lifted Cami onto the saddle.

Houston stood close, keeping a good hand on the toddler. Carley sensed him communicating with the horse, commanding her to stand still. Carley didn't have to guess about Cami's reactions, however. Her daughter loved being on the horse, and she seemed to know instinctively what to do. Cami bucked her bottom and lightly kicked her feet.

Carley walked over to stand on the other side of the horse, close enough to Cami to catch her if anything happened. She looked over Cami's head and caught a glimpse of Houston's enraptured face. He was having more fun than her little girl.

The more Carley watched his amusement, the more she realized she was hungrier for him than she'd thought. Taking a steadying breath, Carley smelled the earthy scent of musky animals mixing with the pungent aroma of hay and manure. She longed to step into her lover's arms and breathe in his own spicy fragrance—the primitive, edgy bouquet of his desire.

She grabbed for the rim of the bristly, horse blanket and fisted her hand around it, trying to stop herself from reaching for Houston. The rough texture against her smooth fingers reminded her of the differences in their bodies. The memory of the wiry hair on his chest as she ran her fingers over his sinewy muscles aroused her to near insanity on the spot.

Carley forced her eyes to focus on Houston as he dragged his gaze from Cami for a second to steal a look at her. "Cami loves this. I'll have to take her for a ride with me sometime." His eyes sparkled with good humor.

"Hmm. Perhaps." Carley tamped down her frustrating needs. She found herself amused at this huge, strong man, who very nearly giggled at Cami's delight. "You're very good with children. I sort of got the impression you weren't fond of babies." She tamed her wayward bodily desires by reminding herself of Cami's presence.

She noticed Houston's first reaction was to shake his head in denial of her words. Then they apparently sank in. He cleared his throat. "I don't think I've had too much experience with the smaller kids. At least, I haven't been comfortable around the little ones for the last eighteen months. But Cami's easy." He matched Carley's gaze over Cami's head. "She's a real charmer, isn't she?"

"Yes, just like her father."

Houston's eyes darkened and his lips straightened to a grim line. He looked from the laughing Cami back to Carley's face then quickly back to Cami. He stayed completely silent for a long moment.

Finally, when Carley thought she'd burst if he didn't say something, he glanced at her again and his features softened into one of his boy-next-door smiles.

"I think you'll be more comfortable letting Cami ride if you know how simple and safe riding is yourself. Why don't I give you a lesson?" he asked.

That was certainly not what Carley had expected him to say. "What? Right now?"

Houston kept his hands on Cami and the horse, but turned his head to check on the other children. The kids were starting to climb up the fence rails and were obviously becoming bored.

"Sure." He grinned at Carley. "As soon as you can get away. No time like the present."

Carley was flustered. Too many thoughts flooded her mind. "Didn't you say you needed some time away from me? Are you positive you want to be alone with me now?"

His smile turned softer, lazy and seductive. "I can't imagine anything nicer than being alone with you. Besides, I may have overreacted some the other night when I said that. I realize now you were only trying to do the right thing." He lifted Cami down off the horse and set her flat on her feet, still keeping one hand firmly on her shoulder.

"I've got lots of questions, Carley, and you're the only one who can give me the answers."

Carley hurried around the big animal and took Cami's hand. "Okay. I guess." Her glance moved to the other caretakers as they picked up their charges and prepared to head back to the main house. "But it's almost lunchtime. I'll have to feed Cami first."

"No problem. It'll take some time to post the kids' afternoon schedules and saddle another horse." Houston looked down at her sandals. "You own any boots?"

"Only dress boots. But they have a pretty little heel."

"Good enough. Put them on and then stop in the kitchen and pick us both up a couple of apples to eat on the trail." He picked the horse's reins off the straw-covered floor. "And get back here as fast as you can. We need to be off before the sun gets much hotter."

Maybe being alone with the seductively sensual Carley and teaching her to ride might not be too smart after all. But when Houston had seen the tenderness on her face as she mentioned Cami's father, he wondered if she'd ever felt those same feelings toward him. Worse yet, he was suddenly desperate to know if she could feel that way toward him now.

Houston shook his head to keep the strong sensations from overtaking him right out here in the open corral. The gelding he'd cut from the rest, then bridled and tied to the fence, gave him an exasperated look. Houston figured he'd better get busy before the horse really started getting antsy. He threw the blanket over the gelding's back and turned to pull the saddle and the rest of the tack off the top fence rail, where he'd placed them earlier.

He'd spent every spare moment over the past hectic, few days mulling over Carley's words—a dangerous preoccupation for a man normally more prone to action. The things she'd told him about his past— the things she hadn't told him—all became more and more worrisome. Like, for instance, what kind of a lawman had he been? Marshall? Policeman? What?

And why had Carley really been the one to come find him? She'd hinted that she was still in law enforcement. Had someone sent her? That particular thought made his mind turn to the darkness again. How had he been hurt, and why? But whenever his thoughts drifted back to the question of why, the pain in his temples became unbearable.

As he'd been playing with Cami and the mare, it occurred to Houston that he might never remember Carley or anything else about his past. Perhaps that wasn't so important anymore. Couldn't he just have a new life, beginning from today? The phrase "Today is the first day of the rest of your life" sprang to mind, and he had to chuckle. Amazing the silly things he could remember, when he couldn't even remember his own name.

If it was possible to start from scratch, he wondered what place Carley and Cami would have in his life. Houston hadn't known them for long, but every instinct told him the three of them somehow belonged together. And if he had been a lawman he'd relied heavily on instinct in his past life. He remembered hearing that at times lawmen used gut reactions in their work.

Well, Houston's gut reaction was to trust in Carley and try for a closer relationship, but he'd better start by asking questions about his past before they discussed the future. Once the whole truth was out, there wouldn't be anything stopping them from starting over. He would just have to pray he could convince Carley.

The biggest stumbling block to convincing her to start over might be the simple fact that every time she came near he lost all rational thought. Whenever he saw Carley the whole world started revolving around his need for the sweetness of her lips or the excitement of her heart beating under his hand.

By the time Carley appeared outside the barn, laden down with a picnic basket big enough to feed the entire staff, Houston had managed to quiet his gnawing concerns and throbbing libido. For some reason he was certain he could trust her to tell him the truth. All he had to do was ask all the right questions.

"Took you long enough." He hefted the basket from her arms and fastened it to his gelding's saddle. "Did Lloyd decide to cook a whole turkey dinner for us?"

"Don't blame Lloyd. Cami started whining the minute she lost sight of you, and then when she figured out I was leaving, she pitched one of the biggest fits of her life."

Her words flowed over him like a warm shower. It didn't matter what she said, he knew his life would be complete if only she would continue to drawl just like that—forever.

"She's a cute kid. I feel the same way about her."

Houston noticed Carley tense at his words. What had he said to cause that reaction? What was she concerned about?

"You ready for your first riding lesson?" The sooner they got started, the sooner he'd be able to ask her all the questions building up inside him.

"I suppose I'm as ready as I'll ever be." Carley marched up to him, spun and faced the horse smack at saddle height. She squared her shoulders and stood at attention. "What do I do first?"

Houston had to laugh. She looked so much like she was about to face a firing squad. "The first thing you can do is relax. The horse won't hurt you. This is the same mare Cami was on. She's the sweetest thing this side of Oklahoma." He took Carley's hand in his and stroked the horse's muzzle.

"Relax. Right." Carley swallowed hard. "Then what? How do I get on this thing?"

Chuckling and without considering the ramifications, he scooped her off her feet and placed her on the mare's back.

Oops. Bad mistake. The feel and smell of the woman assailed his senses with sweet misery.

"First off, don't call her a thing. Her name is Lovey," he managed, backing up a half step.

Carley jerked her head toward him and nearly swung herself out of the saddle. "Lovey?"

"Hold on, there." He fought for a little emotional distance. "Don't fidget around so much till you first plant your feet in the stirrups." Houston forced one of her boots into a stirrup and readjusted the height to fit her. "Sit still while I come around and fix the other one."

"Did you give the horse her name?"

He was busy with the other foot. "What? Yeah, I guess so. We bought her at auction with no papers. Her previous owner had wanted a cattle horse, not a people-loving animal. He'd never bothered to name her and was ready to let her go to the Japanese for horsemeat."

Carley gasped and laid a hand on the mare's long mane. "Horsemeat? Oh, my God. The poor thing."

Houston couldn't stop his broad smile. This woman was more tenderhearted even than Gabe, and Gabe found it difficult to step on ants, for cripe's sake.

"Stop fussing. She'll have a long and happy life here with the kids. The mare loves everybody. That's why I gave her the name." He untied the mare from the fence post and handed Carley the reins.

Carley's eyes softened and she gazed at him quietly for a long minute. "You used to say that same thing about me...that I loved everybody. You've even called me Lovey a time or two."

She spoke so softly that her words didn't knock him over the way they might have. Instead he only felt a vague pain in the vicinity of his heart. "I wish I could remember you, Carley. More than you'll ever know. But I..."

"Don't try too hard. You'll only push the memories away." She blinked once. "Come on. You got me up here on this...Lovey. Let's get on with the lesson."

In one fluid motion Houston mounted his own horse. He waited for the gelding to adjust to his weight, then gave Carley a brief lesson in horsemanship and how to make a horse obey commands.

In no time at all they were riding along the trail, heading toward the river. Carley looked as if she'd been riding all her life. Back straight, head high, she'd found the right "seat" without being taught how to follow the horse's gait.

Houston didn't want to mention it to Carley, but Gabe had heard a rumor that a Mexican *coyote* would be bringing people across the river near the ranch's property. They rode slowly, and Houston thought now might be a good time to look for any sign of new immigrant trails. Fat chance. He couldn't take his eyes from the energetic and dramatic-looking woman riding next to him.

In the sunlight, her loose flowing hair glinted red, and her perky breasts bounced slightly with every step of the horse. Once in a while something new captured her attention, and she bubbled with questions and laughter. Carley made the whole world glitter. Houston's heart grew lighter by the minute. No matter what had happened between them before, nothing could stop them this time around.

As they walked the horses along the riverbank, Carley asked, "Is this the Rio Grande?"

Houston nodded and eyed the far side. "Right here, you can throw a rock and hit Mexico, then wade across and retrieve it. The water's low because of the drought."

"Do you have a problem with Mexican nationals walking across your property?"

"They do come through here sometimes, but it's usually no problem for us. The Border Patrol has the right to watch this area, but they normally do their stake-outs at night. They're busy other places during the daylight hours."

Houston guided his horse up the slight incline and headed toward the *resaca*. "We keep the brush trimmed back along the Rio Grande. There's no place a man can hide for several miles inland."

Carley's docile mare naturally followed behind the gelding. "How would someone go about bringing children across?"

Houston slowed his horse so they could ride side by side. "Lots of ways, I hear tell." He shrugged a shoulder. "Tiny tots are hidden under blankets and coats. Or sometimes they place them on rafts and pull them across on a jury-rigged system of ropes. The bigger kids can wade or swim themselves across." He was about to ask why that was important to her when the sight of the canal and dirt road where he'd been found captured his attention.

"See that road on top of the canal bank over there?" he asked.

Carley nodded and looked over to him for an explanation.

"Right about there was where Doc Luisa found me beaten and shot eighteen months ago." A dark cloud passed over the sun and he shuddered involuntarily. "I was no more than a hundred yards from the Rio Grande, but miles from the nearest house or public road."

"But…what were you doing way out here?"

He shrugged his shoulders. "That's a question we'd all like answered."

Carley's gaze shifted suddenly as she caught sight of the willows and live oak trees surrounding the *resaca,* about a half mile away. "Oh, look, it's beautiful and so peaceful. Is that part of the river way over there?"

"Nope. At one time it was part of the river. In the past, the entire area has flooded over many times." Houston raised his arm in an arch, indicating the whole range within view. "Each time the Rio Grande receded, these little river-like lakes were left behind. The Mexican word for them is *resaca.*"

Houston rode up under a willow's branches and dismounted. "Stay on Lovey until I have a good grip on her.'' He grounded his horse's reins and took hold of the mare's bridle.

Carley looked first on one side of the horse and then the other. "It's awfully high up here, isn't it?"

"Hold on. I forgot you haven't learned how to dismount yet." He tied Lovey's reins to a willow reed. The spindly little brush wouldn't hold a difficult horse, but Houston knew he wouldn't have to worry about the gentle mare.

In two steps he was at Carley's side. "Step down hard in the stirrup with your left foot while you swing your right leg up an over the horse's tail. Hang on to the saddle, pull your left foot out and ease to the ground.''

Carley tried to do as he'd instructed but hesitated, holding all her weight on her left leg. Her back was to him as she faced the saddle and panicked. He placed his hands around her waist, hoping to steady her and give her the courage to slide both feet to the ground.

Instead of letting go, she kept her left foot in the stirrup and tried to ease her right leg down toward solid earth. Her foot soon twisted and caught in the stirrup. She quickly overbalanced. Lost and stuck, her backside hit Houston's mid-section.

At the first connection of her body with his, every nerve went on alert. At once, he moved to grasp her higher up. As his fingers grazed her rib cage, the muscles in his chest and gut clenched.

Slowly—achingly slow—she inched down his body. As her rounded bottom passed over the strain in his jeans, the most pleasurable pain he could re-

member made him grow harder than ever. Sweat began forming in the small of his back, and the buzzing
in his ears wasn't coming from swarming insects.

Houston opened his mouth to ask her if she was
doing all right and found his throat dry. Something
had to give soon, so finally he managed a few raspy
words. "You'd better plant both your feet on the
ground right now or I can't guarantee we'll ever get
to lunch."

Houston stepped away from Carley's body, fighting
the fog clouding his judgment. The same overwhelming need that had dogged him on the dance floor the
other night turned his brains to mush once again. A
primitive desire to link his body to hers in an ageless,
sexual dance throbbed through his veins, setting his
teeth on edge and forcing him to take a deep breath
in his effort at control.

Man, oh, man, the two of them must have been
some hot item when they were lovers in the past. The
simmering lust was obvious, as well as nearly impossible to overcome.

Carley found firm footing and eased around to face
him. Her eyes darkened and the lids nearly closed.
When she bestowed a shy, come-to-me kind of smile
on him, he knew she'd felt the same thrust of passion
that had overtaken him.

She said nothing, but raised her arms, begging him
to step into her embrace. Houston swallowed a giant
lump in his throat and took another step backward.

Not here. Not yet. There was too much he had to
know.

When he coughed and shook his pants leg out to

adjust the pressure, Carley widened her eyes and dropped her hands to her side. The moment of need passed—slowly.

Houston opened his saddle bags and pulled from them a couple of heavy horse blankets and a tarp. He moved farther under the willows, closer to the river, all the while checking the ground for a smooth spot to sit. He'd picked this place to stop because he knew no fire ants or killer bees would be nearby to ruin their picnic.

Houston intended to ask all his questions before he succumbed to the erotic drive pounding inside him. He silently vowed that before the day was over, he'd know all about his past—and all about every inch of Carley, as well.

Eight

Carley filled her lungs with sweet, country air and plopped herself down in the middle of one of the blankets. Houston headed back to the horses after he'd helped remove her boots. She flipped the hair off the back of her neck, letting the air cool her body. Settling down, she watched Houston give the horses a drink from the *resaca*. In short order he'd retied the mare in the shade and unloaded the basket from the gelding.

Her senses were so highly strung from the nearness of the man she loved that the world around Carley took on a surreal quality. She wiggled her toes and inhaled deeply. The aroma of the place enthralled her, and she tried to pick out the differing scents. There were the odors of the animals and the earth she sat on, of course. They weren't totally unpleasant, only rugged and natural.

Other fragrances titillated her senses, as well. Smells of musk, flowering weeds and the tangy perfume of sweat. Ah, heady stuff. It was good to be a woman in love and in tune with nature on a day as fine and clear as this one.

Houston lowered the basket to the blanket in front of her and caught her gaze. Her total contentment with the place and the company must have shone in her face, because his apprehensive look quickly turned to pleasure, only slightly shadowed by a pensive quality.

"Like it out here, huh?" He peeled off his Stetson and bent to one knee. "I'm glad. I come here alone sometimes to think, but the *resaca* is several feet lower than usual and clogged with those nasty weeds."

Carley's heart skittered, beating wildly at the sight of his grin and the lone lock of hair falling over his forehead. "I don't think of hyacinths as weeds. They have pretty flowers sometimes." She looked to the right and to the left. "This little river is landlocked anyway. With no rain how does it ever get any water?"

"An irrigation channel," he answered. "But with the drought, they're using the water for other purposes."

She was finding it hard to concentrate so Carley decided to do something useful with her hands. "Let's see what Lloyd packed for us." She reached out for the basket.

Food wasn't what she needed right now, but if the man was hungry, Carley's basic instinct was to fill her man's stomach so he could concentrate on other things. "Here, let me." She dug into the basket. "I watched Lloyd pack the basket while I was feeding Cami.''

"Looks like Lloyd got carried away. Did he think we were bringing all the kids along?''

Carley pulled out the small but sturdy plastic cooler. "I don't believe he would've packed this for the children." She handed Houston the cooler. "Open a couple of these while I unpack the food."

With a questioning look, Houston opened the cooler and smiled. "Ah, beer. Good old Lloyd. Wonder where he had it stashed? Gabe doesn't exactly approve of alcohol in the house." He started to pull apart a couple of cans. "You want beer or a soda?''

Carley pointed to a soda and kept digging through the basket.

"I'll push a few of those water lilies aside and put the cooler into the *resaca*. That'll help keep the rest of the cans cold." He walked back to the horses and pulled a length of rope from a saddle pack.

As he stood next to the horses, Carley noticed how powerful and steady the animals were. Just like the man, she thought.

She found herself gawking at his well-built body, lean and long, as he strode to the edge of the water. Carley decided Houston's muscles had become more defined since he'd been working on the ranch. The man she'd been partnered with had kept himself in shape by working out, but this man's hard-earned physique reeked of potency and sex.

Whew! Carley felt herself flush, and the day suddenly seemed warmer…more humid than a minute ago. Thinking back to when she'd slid off the horse, she vividly remembered running her backside over his chest and down past his metal belt-buckle, finally finding the hardness of his desire for her. When he'd stepped away, she'd tried to put it out of her mind. But now...

"You all right? The heat getting to you?" Houston kneeled on the edge of the blanket and popped the top off the soda. "You'd better have something cold to drink." He handed her the icy can. Avoiding her gaze, he sat and tugged off his boots.

Carley took a gulp. "I'm fine." She struggled for clarity of thought and speech. "I do think maybe I'll take my long-sleeved shirt off."

She'd deliberately worn a bright-red tank top under her long-sleeved Western shirt in case the day turned warmer. And it certainly had. As she dragged her arms from the sleeves, she realized the warmth wasn't because of the weather.

Throwing the shirt aside and pulling the first of the sandwiches from the basket, Carley found she needed the distraction of food to keep her from making a fool of herself. "Let's see what we have in here." She swallowed hard in an effort to steady her voice. "Want the barbecued brisket or the egg salad?"

"Either."

"Fine. You take the..." She lifted her head and held out the clear-plastic wrapped sandwich to him. When she caught his gaze, she found his hungry eyes roaming over her body rather than looking at the object in her hand. "...brisket," she finished.

Her stomach fluttered, reminding her of the lemon-colored butterfly that zipped past moments ago. Like the hibiscus opening its buds at first light, her body responded to the warm look she found in his eyes. When Houston didn't even try to disguise his desire, her nipples puckered with stinging prickles of sensation.

Houston took the sandwich from her hand. "We'd better eat." He focused his gaze somewhere over her shoulder and took a bite of brisket. "I've thought of some questions for you, and I'd like to get them asked before it gets too hot for us to stay out here."

As far as Carley was concerned, it was already too hot. But if the man trusted her enough to want to ask questions, then far be it from her to discourage him. Slowly and deliberately she unpacked the bounty Lloyd had assembled. From the depths of the basket, she pulled cheeses, pickles, stuffed jalapeños, fruit and cookies to go along with the sandwiches and drinks.

Carley couldn't have cared less about eating, but to her everlasting surprise they polished off the bulk of the lunch in companionable silence. Still hungry for spicier things, she lay back on the blanket and looked at the clear, azure sky through the branches of the willow.

From the corner of her eye, she watched as Houston left an apple on the blanket between them and packed up the rest of the trash. In his bare feet, he returned the basket to the horses and stopped to pull a couple more cans from the water before dropping down next to her again.

He set the cans down unopened, stretched out on his side, propped his head on his hand and studied her profile.

"Tell me about your background. Who are you really, Charleston Mills?"

Carley smiled, buying time to gather her thoughts. "I was born in Charleston, South Carolina, obviously.

It was my father's hometown and he'd just turned his family's business there into a huge conglomerate.'' She turned on her side to face Houston. "He was brilliant, a high-tech geek…before that was cool. Chester Mills had carrot-red hair and sky-blue eyes covered over with thick, horn-rimmed glasses.''

Carley hesitated, thinking of the man she'd never gotten a chance to know. "And he loved my mother with a passion to rival Rhett Butler's. My father died in an automobile accident six months after I was born.''

"Carley…is it hard to talk about him?''

She discovered she couldn't look into his eyes when they were filled with compassion. It hurt her sensitive soul, so she flopped on her back again and concentrated on the puffy clouds passing overhead.

"I never knew him, so actually…I like talking about him. It keeps his memory alive for me. While I was growing up, my mother spent hours telling me everything about him. To this day he seems so real I can hardly believe he's not around.'' She swallowed, then breathed a sigh.

"My mother, on the other hand, has always been way too real. Mom's a Creole, born and raised in New Orleans. I inherited my looks from her.'' She ran her fingers through her thick hair. "All except this rust-colored mop on my head. Anyway, when Mom found herself a young widow with a baby, she packed me up and went home. My grandparents took us in.''

Carley lazily sat up, facing her former lover. "Of course, it didn't hurt anything that Dad had left her rich. Mom's what you might call 'earthy.' Sensual. She doesn't come alive until men pay attention.''

"I think maybe you inherited a good portion of that from her, too."

"Why, I do believe that's one of the nicest things you've ever said to me, Houston Smith," Carley murmured in her best femme-fatale accent.

When Houston scowled, she laughed and continued. "Mom is on her fourth husband now, I think. My grandparents raised me. Maybe 'doted on me' might be a better choice of words."

Houston pulled himself upright, crossed his legs in front of him and reached for the apple. Carley found herself grabbing for it at the same time. Their hands touched—and lingered.

Carley deliberately lowered her lashes and stayed silent. Both of them were frozen, suspended in a sexual tug-of-war. She raised her lids slowly and let the narcotic pull she'd sensed in his smile show in her eyes.

"Some say I was spoiled. I prefer to think it's just that people like me well enough to let me have whatever I want." She pinned him with as dreamy a look as she could muster and heard her own smoky tone begging him for what she needed. "What do you think?"

Houston dropped his half of the apple as if it had burned him, but he never took his eyes off her. "I think you could probably get anything you set your heart on." He watched her put the apple to her lips and take a bite, while her eyes studied him with a dancing twinkle of amusement.

Yeah. No question. He'd gladly give her anything she wanted.

But not just yet.

"Tell me how we met." A part of Houston ached

to kiss her senseless. Another part of him wanted to protect his soul from the hurt that had haunted him for the past year and a half. He wanted to trust someone, to depend on someone, and he desperately wanted that someone to be the beautiful and sexy woman who drew him to her like a magnet.

Carley's bottom lip curled into a pout, and she set the apple aside. Apparently, food wasn't what she'd had her heart set on this time.

"You'd been a special agent for about six years when the Bureau recruited me after graduate school. You pitched a fit when your new supervisor sprung a woman partner on you."

"Agent? I was an FBI special agent?"

"Hmm. You sure made the mental jump from 'Bureau' to 'FBI' in a hurry. But yes, after a stint in the service you became an agent in the Houston field office." She scrutinized his face. "You were furious about being saddled with a woman. You barely spoke to me."

He'd heard some of what she was saying between the lines. "You were an agent, too?"

Carley smiled but her eyes were grim. "I still am an FBI agent, Houston. I'm also a child psychologist like I told you. I'm here in the valley…on special assignment."

"Am I your special assignment?" To his own ears, his voice sounded hoarse, rough. Every fiber of his being prayed he'd find the peace he'd been seeking with every new revelation.

She lowered her eyes again. "Only partially." Carley pushed a strand of hair behind her ear. "After about a month together as partners, we had to requalify on the special-weapons range. You bet me a bottle of champagne that you'd score better than I did.'' She lifted her chin and smiled at him once more. ''You lost.''

Her eyes took on a dreamy, drowsy quality, as if she were lost in her memories. Houston opened his mouth to speak and had to expel the breath he found he'd been holding. He shut his eyes against the need that slammed into him. The absolute *want* of Carley constricted his lungs and sped blood to his loins. In just a few days she'd become his everything: the beating of his pulse, the connection to his past, the only thing that mattered about his future.

His free hand moved to cover hers. ''I hope I was a good sport about it.''

Carley snorted. ''Hah! I had to badger you into making good on the bet. Then, when I couldn't pop the cork on the magnum and had to ask you to do it for me…well, we both ended up with more champagne on us than in the glasses.''

She chuckled low in her throat, and Houston watched the edge of her top rise and fall against the soft swell of her breast as she breathed.

''We were so absurd, standing there soaking wet and fuming—'' her eyes lost their focus again and she absently threaded her fingers through his ''—we broke down in gales of laughter. From then on, we became real partners and good friends.''

''Friends?''

Her mouth curved into a seductive smile and she licked her bottom lip. He sat up to face her and placed his free hand against her cheek. Her skin was soft—satiny smooth.

The delicate curve of her jaw drew his attention down her neck to the pulse point at the base. A searing need to place his lips just there and taste the throb of her heart pounded through his veins—hard. He didn't trust himself to do what his body demanded. His emotions were too strong, touching him deeply— in a place half-forgotten.

She shook her head, blinked and continued speaking, her voice softening. "Friends…for about a year. Then we were sent on a difficult, late-night surveillance." Her voice had a hypnotic quality that seeped inside his skin and wound tightly around his libido.

"We set ourselves and our recording equipment up comfortably in a butler's pantry and waited. One of the suspects was late, so the others decided to enjoy themselves while they waited for their comrade. They ended up partying all night." Her eyes told the story her lips wouldn't tell. "So did we, in our own quiet way."

Houston felt as though he was rushing toward a cliff, bound and determined to throw himself over the side. He had no business touching and wanting any woman as badly as he wanted Carley. He felt a desperate hunger to have her—wanted to devour her whole.

Houston looked down and realized his hands were shaking. Slowly, unsteadily, he framed both his hands on each side of her face and leaned in for a kiss. He promised himself, just one brush of her lips, then he could regain his control.

But as his lips caressed hers and he tasted strawberries, oatmeal cookies and sweet, womanly musk, a wildfire erupted inside him. Carley clung to him, and her sweetness turned to sultry, pulsating pleasure—rich and earthy. One last coherent thought pulled him back, but he couldn't resist nibbling on the corners of her mouth.

"I'm sorry I don't remember any of this, Carley. And I'm more than sorry if my disappearance caused you any trouble. Maybe we could start new?"

When he gazed down into her eyes, he was pleased to see them darkened with desire. Her breath came in little pants and she looked as if she'd been fighting for the same control he'd tried to find.

"First, let me explain about Cami. When you disappeared…"

"No! I don't want to know anything about Cami's father." The surprising stroke of jealousy caught him unawares and defenseless. The thought of any other man touching Carley, kissing her, pouring his seed inside her made him want to put his fist through the tree. "She's a bright and beautiful child that any man should be proud to claim. But right now I've had enough talk."

Right now her lips were slightly swollen from his kiss and were the rosy color of a smoldering fire. Houston longed to dance once again in the flames. His hands tingled with the need to touch her skin, fill his palms with her firm breasts.

He couldn't hold back, he simply had to taste the succulent fruit that was all Carley. He swayed toward her and lightly kissed her once more.

"Charleston," he managed against her lips.

Houston sank deep into the velvet softness of her mouth. She made a slight noise, feline and low, like a purr, and all rational thought oozed out of his brain. Her body fitted to his as if they'd been made together.

Struggling to be fair to her, to give her a chance to halt the inevitable conclusion to the way things were headed, he backed off and tried a smile. Carley's look was confused—shocked.

"But…but I…" she stammered.

"Did I kiss you wrong? Wasn't it the way you remembered?" His brain was fogged and he felt dizzy.

"No, it was…" She pulled at his shoulders and dragged him down for another mind-blowing kiss.

Her lips scorched his, and he filled his mouth with her silken tongue. Meanwhile a certainty of purpose filled the rest of him. Being with Carley was right. They belonged in each other's arms. He hadn't felt so sure of anything since the amnesia.

"Were we always this hot together?" he murmured against her temple while he took a shaky breath.

Houston kissed his way down her jawline, lightly skimming over satin skin as he made his way to the base of her neck and the throbbing pulse that awaited him. Carley threw her head back, giving him an open path to travel.

"Did I always need to pause right here to feel your pulse under my lips?" He sucked gently as Carley moaned. His hands rubbed lightly over her back then moved to her rib cage.

He continued kissing her neck and shoulders while his hands roamed under her top, dancing lightly over her skin. When he realized she'd worn no bra, he froze.

Shuddering, he left his hands on the sides of her breasts and pulled back to look at her. Her nipples peaked, pushing against the thin material, and under his inspection a reddish glow worked up from the base of her neck, capturing her throat. There wasn't anything he could do to stop himself from pulling her top up and over her head.

She raised her arms for him and lowered her eyelids. He leaned back once more and let his gaze wander over the beauty that was Carley, over the generous and perfectly formed breasts with their dusky tips begging for his attention.

"You're a goddess." Because she stayed perfectly still and simply gazed into his eyes, he filled his hands with her firm flesh. Her rounded curves molded into his palms, and he kneaded her breasts as carefully as he could, considering how desperate he was to ravage her.

Her eyes turned to deep jade as she bit on her lower lip.

"Charleston, love. I'm nearly blinded by my need for you. But if you want to stop, tell me now."

Instead of answering him, she reached to undo his shirt buttons. He helped her tear his shirt off, and she flung it behind her. When she flattened her hands on his bare chest, Carley closed her eyes and growled. Low deep and guttural. The kitten she had been turned to savage cat.

Houston bent to suckle one of her nipples while gently rolling the other tip in his fingers. He leaned her back against the blanket and nudged one of his knees between her legs. Blowing lightly, he delicately licked the peak of the nipple he'd been teasing and moved to the other. When he kissed the puckered tip and drew it deep into his mouth, Carley began to squirm under him.

She dug her fingers through his hair and pulled his head closer to her chest, holding him to her. Houston could feel the sweat trickling down his spine as he held back, not wanting to rush her.

He stroked his hand over her thigh and placed the heel of his palm against the juncture of her legs. Carley's breath hitched and her hands flew to the waistband of his jeans, fumbling against the tough material. In a flurry of hands and moans, they made short work of the rest of their clothes.

Houston knelt in front of her. Truly a goddess, her hair billowed around her like a cloud. He tried desperately to keep from rushing. But when her golden skin, the color of warm nectar, shimmered in the gentle sunlight, he lost most of his resolve.

Carley lay back against the ground and raised pleading arms to him, her eyes aflame with arousal. He kept his gaze on hers, but let his hands move to her inner thighs, where the skin was as soft as a kitten's fur. As Houston touched her, he saw the luminosity in her eyes burning brighter. When he skimmed his fingers across the downy covering to her inner core, she closed her eyes and arched her back.

He was insane. Driven mad by an animal need to possess this woman. To drive himself so deep within her that nothing before or after would ever matter.

Houston bent to taste her belly button and eased a finger into her wet, welcoming warmth. Carley's hips lifted off the blanket, and when he looked at her face, her lips had parted. She softly moaned on each sharp, panting breath. His own breathing seemed loud in his ears, and the blood coursing through his veins sounded like the roaring whoosh of shallow river rapids.

Gently he parted her legs, giving himself more room to maneuver, and kissed a path down her belly.

With one finger still deep inside her, he used the flat of his tongue to flick across her inflamed nub. Carley jerked, mouthed a keening wail, and Houston felt the ripples of completion thundering through her.

Houston's own body was trembling and aching beyond belief, but after he'd held her until she'd stilled, he moved to pick up his jeans.

Carley opened her eyes and lifted a hand to touch him. "What are you doing? Come to me."

He clamped a hand tightly around her wrist and stopped her from closing her fingers around his rigid shaft. His hands were shaking so badly he was afraid he'd embarrass himself. Finally he dug the foil packet from his pocket and ripped it open.

"What...?" She lifted her head and watched him unroll the condom to cover himself.

He managed a tight smile. "Good old Doc Luisa. Thank God she left her health class materials at the ranch."

"You...you're protecting us?" Her eyes were wild and nearly black with desire.

"Not from any disease. Doc gave me plenty of blood tests, and I haven't been with a woman since...before I can remember." He moved to kneel beside her. "And it isn't your health I'm concerned about, either. It's just that a man needs to protect the woman he intends to...love. When we make children together, it'll be because we both want them and intend to raise them as a family."

Carley groaned, low and deep, and Houston suddenly feared he'd said the wrong thing. He certainly didn't want to remind her of Cami's father. Maybe he had.

He leaned over her and placed a tender kiss on her lips. "Want to change your mind?"

"You…you'd let me back out now? But you…you haven't—" She raised her head to question him.

"You're the boss here, my love. This is all for you. All you have to do is say no."

Carley threw her head back on the blanket. "Yes!" She shut her eyes and reached for him.

Houston chuckled and, breathing a sigh of relief, moved to cover her with his body. He placed his elbows on either side of her head and leaned on them, staring down at her beautiful face.

"Open your eyes, Carley. I need to see that you're doing okay."

Her eyes popped open as he reached one hand down between their bodies, testing her readiness. He found moisture and heat, and dropped his head to take one of her breasts into his mouth. While he sucked deeply on her inflamed tip, he let his hardened length nudge the entrance to her hot, liquid comfort, but halted before entering.

Despite the rage inside him, he had to be sure. "Last chance, Carley."

She gripped his shoulders and dug her nails into his skin, setting fires where she touched. "Please. Oh, please." Her cry was more than a request. It was a demand, and Houston fully intended to meet her need and his own.

He gripped her buttocks with his hands and, on a slow agonizing slide, entered her cavern. She gasped and threw her legs around his waist, sending him deeper. Houston heard himself groan with the overwhelming pleasure of it. Carley bit into his shoulder and made small, guttural sounds, like an animal—feral and wild.

And Houston knew everything was the way it should be. This was where he belonged.

He let himself go then, as he pulled her violently to him, thrusting madly, setting their fast-paced tempo. Carley matched his speed and arched into him, grinding her hips against his. When he knew she was coming apart again in his arms, he threw his head back and silently thanked God for the power that existed between them.

As the world spun on its axis, Houston shuddered into her one last time and vowed he'd never leave her again.

They collapsed together and fought to regulate their breathing. Their skin, slick with sweat, began to cool in the caress of the gentle warm breeze. Carley held him tight, and he lifted his head to kiss her forehead.

Houston tenderly pushed aside a strand of damp hair matted to her cheek. That's when he first noticed the stream of tears, dripping from the corners of her closed eyes. A small sob bubbled from her throat.

Good Lord, he thought. His love, his life…must be in pain, and it had to be all his fault.

Nine

"Oh, God. I've hurt you somehow." Houston rolled to his side, keeping Carley tucked close to him. "Are you in pain? Was it something I said?"

Carley had never felt so idiotic in her life. What the heck was she supposed to tell the man? That she'd just made love to a complete stranger? That she'd been foolish enough to believe that Houston Smith would behave exactly as he had before he'd lost his memory? Or that, the real pain had come when she discovered she'd fallen in love with a man who only resembled her former lover in a vaguely physical way.

The stress of this whole thing must have driven her crazy. Surely only a crazed woman would be praying for an injured man to stay injured—to have amnesia forever.

She tried to sit up, but Houston's muscled forearm pinned her in place. "I'm fine," Carley mumbled, and swiped at her eyes with the back of her hand. "Let me up."

"Honey, talk to me...please." He leaned his forehead against hers and tenderly ran his thumb up under her eyelashes, brushing away the stinging, hot tears that refused to stop.

Carley bit down on her bottom lip, hoping the new pain would hide the tear in her heart. She felt like a liar and a cheat. Cheating on a man whose very memory had kept her alive for a year an a half. And son-of-a-gun, if she hadn't cheated on him with... with...him!

"All right. If you can't tell me what's wrong, then I'll talk. You listen." He placed a gentle kiss on her temple and kept his hand on her cheek, running his thumb over the wet streaks, then over her swollen lips.

Carley tasted her own salty tears and felt a chill as her body began to cool down. Her mind raced, trying to find some shading on the truth that Houston might believe. She damned herself for not having lied in the beginning. She could have told him they were married. Then she wouldn't have to worry about Cami, or worry about him having become another person. None of it would matter. She could just keep him in the dark. And just—keep him.

"When I first came around after my injury, the world seemed terrifying and dangerous. I couldn't trust anyone." Houston whispered low and soft in her ear. "I imagined that either someone would show up to finish the job they'd started or I'd wake up some morning and the whole thing would have been a bad dream."

He swallowed hard and tightened his grip on her.

"As the days turned into weeks, and the weeks turned into months, the fear of the unknown began to take a back seat to loneliness. I longed to find some link to my past, to find someone who'd cared about me."

He took a deep breath and smiled against her cheek. "You can't imagine how lonely you can be when everyone else has a story to tell about their families or their childhood, and you have nothing to say. It makes you a nonperson, a man without love or hate. A man with nothing."

Carley turned on her side to face him. He spoke so softly, so smoothly, she had to look at him. He'd been through so much. You could see it in the many new scars that angrily marked his body, and in the new look of desperation in his eyes.

"Then you showed up, and everything felt so familiar. At first I was afraid to trust you, but every time you smiled it was like the echo of an old song running through my brain. Then I was afraid to trust my own emotions. I figured maybe I'd just latched on to you like a life preserver…like I would have done with anything that came from my past. But the connection between us is strong, pulling us together no matter what. I must've loved you very much in my past life, Charleston Mills."

Her tears had dried. She knew it because they were about to start all over again. The man that Houston used to be had never said he'd loved her. Witt Davidson couldn't have managed to talk about any emotion, let alone discuss their relationship. Carley knew that was the reason he'd never thought to protect them when making love. Witt couldn't admit to himself that they were, indeed, in love.

"When you're with me, it doesn't matter so much

if I ever get my memories back. I want to start our relationship from scratch.'' Houston's eyes looked deep into her soul. ''You're a mighty powerful aphrodisiac, my love. I can't be around you for two minutes without wanting to run my fingers through your hair and wrap myself in your warm comfort.''

Carley had to touch him. His gaze drew her closer, and she touched her lips to his while running her fingers through all that thick, straw-colored hair. As she moved in closer to his body, Carley's senses electrified when she found him hard and eager for her again. She closed her eyes and shuddered with anticipation.

Houston put a finger under her chin and lifted, forcing her to open her eyes. ''But I won't rush you. I know I lost you once before, but I don't want you to think about the past now. I don't want to scare you or hurt you. I want you to be sure of me this time. I won't ever leave you again, I promise.''

Cherished.

That was the word on the tip of her tongue. The man treated her like a priceless treasure, and here she was feeling like some wanton, shameless hussy for not telling him the whole truth.

Confused.

That might be a better word for the state of her brain. Confused by tenderness, kindness and quiet concern.

Houston moved his hands to her waist and, in a flash, had her turned away from him and sitting in his lap. Carley felt the springy curls of hair on his chest as they tickled her back. She leaned into him, assailed by his hard arousal pressing into her buttocks—setting off fireworks inside her. She tried to turn back to face him, but he held her in place.

"Talk to me," he murmured on a breathy whisper in her ear. "Tell me more about us."

She couldn't speak, and wouldn't know what to say if she did.

He didn't wait for her to reply. "Do my fingers feel the same on your skin?" Houston stroked her breasts with gentle touches—almost reverently.

Carley sucked in a deep breath, trying to swallow around the lump in her throat. He cupped her breasts, and his wicked hands teased her nipples.

"Uh…" She found her mouth going dry, washed out along with the thoughts in her brain.

"Do my lips burn your skin the way they used to? The same way yours do mine?" He bent to place branding kisses on the back of her neck, her shoulders. Carley reached her hands over her head to grab fistfuls of his hair, arching her body and giving him better access.

As one of Houston's hands continued to flick over her breasts, the other moved to her belly—soothing, caressing. "Your body comes alive when I touch you. Was it always this way?"

Her body burned like liquid heat, intensifying the ache between her legs. Carley moaned, low and sultry, her own voice foreign to her ears.

"Do you like having my hands on you now, my love?"

"Yes," she gasped, and his hand moved to her warm wetness.

He stoked the inside of her thighs. "Did you like my hands on you before?"

Carley squirmed again, desperate to face him, to sink into his embrace. But Houston held her fast. He drove her farther, higher than she'd ever been. There was no before, no after, only now. Only this man. Only Houston.

"Did you love me then?" His voice was scratchy, needy in her ear.

How could she tell him what was in her heart? The only thing she ever wanted between them from now on was the truth. "I can't lie to you. I did think I loved you, but you…"

Her words lodged in her throat as his hands stilled. Suddenly she was facing him, but not too sure how she got there. He gripped her shoulders, pinning her again.

Houston's eyes were a flashing thunderstorm of color, his breath came in short pants. "I can't hear this yet. I went back on my word, didn't I? I said I wouldn't rush you, and then I pushed."

Carley's head was swimming. She fisted her hands against his chest and tried to clear the fog in her brain. "No. No. You don't understand. Give me a chance…"

"I do understand, but you have to give me a chance…to make it up to you." He grinned at her, like a little, lost boy trying to find his way home. "Let's begin all over again, starting with a date. I want to bring you flowers, take you dancing, maybe even park down by the river and neck."

"Sounds nice." But there isn't much time left. With every tick of the clock, the time remaining for their last chance sped away.

Houston got to his feet, dragging her with him. He swung her up in his arms. "Nice? Nice?" His face screwed up in a scowl. "I want wonderful. I want passionate. I want to make new dreams. I don't want 'nice.'"

She couldn't help the giggle that burst from her lips. He was so alive.

He took a few steps in the direction of the *resaca,* the gleam in his eyes becoming mischievous.

"What do you think you're doing? Where are you taking me?"

"I think it's time we cooled off our relationship...so we can start fresh."

She squirmed, trying to escape his grip, but it was no use. "Don't you dare do what you have in mind. I'm a grown woman. A mother, for heaven's sake," she squeaked in protest. "Stop, or I'll never speak to..."

Carley swore she'd never before seen a look of pure joy like the one shining on Houston's face. He whooped once and stepped off a short ledge, plunging them both feet-first into the midst of the hyacinth-clogged water.

God. Keeping his hands off Carley might be the hardest thing he'd ever done in his life—at least what he could remember of his life.

Houston dragged them both out of the *resaca* and quickly pulled on his jeans. He began using his old work shirt to dry her off. That's when he realized that telling her they could start over again would be a lot easier than convincing his body.

He made a couple of quick swipes at her back. The second time his knuckles connected with silky, smooth skin he dropped his hands to his side.

"Here." He shoved his shirt at Carley. "Dry off the best you can. We need to get back to the ranch." His voice sounded sharper than he'd intended.

She took the shirt and began rubbing her arms. "Your shirt's gonna be soaked."

Carley looked up at him and smiled one of her sexy, let-me-satisfy-your-every-desire smiles. She was so beautiful. Tiny droplets of water beaded on her golden skin and clung to her dark eyelashes. The water had slicked back her hair when he'd pulled her up on the shore behind him. Now the wet strands hung down her back, creating little rivulets that trickled their way over that exquisite expanse of bare skin.

Sensuous, steamy satin.

Houston had to shove his hands into his back pockets to keep them off her. He knew now, for sure, what it felt like to bury himself in all that comforting warmth, to join with her—body, mind and soul. How the heck would he manage to look at Carley and not touch? To be with her and keep his distance?

When she bent over to pick up her clothes, Houston caught a glimpse of those impossibly long legs, ending at the round contours of her uncovered bottom. He swung around and headed for the horses so fast he nearly bumped into the willow. Hopefully, when she had her clothes on, it would be easier to stand his ground.

He fiddled with the basket and the horse blankets, trying to give her time. Houston needed to find something else to talk to her about. Something besides their old relationship.

He'd given it a lot of thought. Judging from his blurry dreams of the dark lady, he must have left Carley for another woman before he'd disappeared. No wonder she'd jumped into the arms of another man and made a baby.

Just the fleeting thought of another man taking her

in his arms, holding her while she cried, watching her while she dressed, made him angry. Not at Carley— at himself for having been stupid enough to let her go.

Well, it wouldn't happen a second time. Now that he'd found her, he wasn't ever letting go again. He only had to be careful not to push her away.

"Thanks." Carley handed him his shirt. "I'm afraid it's wet enough to wring out."

"Don't worry about it." He shoved his arms in the sleeves and forced his eyes to focus on something else besides her. "It'll dry before we get back to the ranch. You ready to go?"

"Yes…"

He heard an expectant hesitation in her voice. Did she want him to say something about what they'd just done? Something about their sensational, mind-blowing afternoon of sex? Houston wasn't sure he could talk about it just yet. If he said anything now, he knew it would lead right back to where his body longed to be. And where he knew he couldn't go. Not today. Not until he'd won back her love.

"Look, Carley…" Houston turned to face her and found her struggling with the wrong foot in the stirrup. Of course. He'd never shown her how to mount a horse. Thank heaven that's all she needed from him.

Houston moved up behind her. "Wrong foot." He tapped the thigh of her other leg, then jerked his hand away. How could he get her on the horse without touching her?

He eased back a pace. "Face the horse. Put your left boot into that stirrup, then pull yourself up by holding on to the saddle horn." When she frowned, he stepped around to hold the horse's bridle. "I'll hold the mare steady. You can do it."

And she did. On the first try. *Damn.* She was spectacular.

They rode along the river in companionable silence, enjoying the hot afternoon sun as it slowly dried their hair and skin. Houston managed to get his body back into the state of half arousal he'd been living with since Carley first showed up.

Side by side. That's how he wanted the rest of their lives to be. Whatever he remembered, or didn't remember, Houston wanted the remainder of his time on earth to be spent taking care of Carley and Cami. He could foresee endless days of teaching Cami about ranch life—and endless nights of teaching her mother the joys of being well and truly loved.

Hell. He was thinking about her again. Houston had to shift in the saddle to rearrange his jeans and give himself time to cool off.

Carley must have sensed he was in discomfort, because she broke the silence that had grown around them. "I kind of expected you to ask me questions about your job with the Bureau. Aren't you curious about what you did?"

"Some," he mumbled. "It makes sense out of my dreams, though. When you said the word *bureau,* a picture of a badge with the words Federal Bureau of Investigation flashed in my mind. I'd seen it many times in my dreams, but figured it was in a whole other context."

He closed his eyes and smiled. "Putting pieces of memories together backward, I originally thought I'd been on the wrong side of seeing that badge."

Houston swiveled in the saddle to look at Carley's

profile. "You, by any chance, know a guy who's big and broad, with a crooked nose and black, soulless eyes?"

Carley threw her head back and laughed. "Sure do. He's our boss, Reid Sorrels. He was the quarterback on his college team. The nose was broken years ago, but he won't talk about it. And the eyes are sharp and black, but soulless? No, he's tough, but the man has a heart under all the gruff."

"Yeah, he sounds like a real pussycat, all right. He's been a big star in some of my nightmares."

Carley leaned across the few feet separating their horses and laid a gentle hand on his arm. "Reid has been a good friend. He stepped in when you disappeared and helped me through some bad times. He's always been a fair boss, but I know he won't rest until we figure out what happened."

"Believe me, I'd like that, too." Houston rubbed at his temples, feeling the searing pain once more. He'd begun to hope he'd felt the last of that particular ache. Guess not. Maybe it wouldn't go away for good until he had all his answers.

"Do you need immediate assistance, Special Agent Mills?" Reid Sorrels's secretary had answered his private line. Carley knew that meant her boss was in the field.

"No. Can you tell me where Reid can be reached?"

"Sorry, no. He said he would be on the move for a couple of days. I understand that one of the baby couriers we have in custody gave him a lead to one of the main kidnappers. Someone on our side of the border, near your vicinity, I believe. You can try

Reid's pager if you like, but he might not be able to get back to you right away."

Carley thanked the woman for her help and clicked off her field-issue, digital phone. She puffed out her cheeks in frustration. Her boss had already moved against his target. That meant many differing things to Carley, and she tried to sort through them.

First off, she only had a couple more days to figure out what she wanted to do about Houston Smith. With no background to rely on, he'd made himself a new set of rules to live by, and they'd caused him to make some faulty assumptions about her and Cami. Now Carley had to decide when and how to tell him the truth. If she did, it would have to be soon. The longer she let him go on thinking she'd had a rebound love affair that had led to Cami's birth, the worse it would be when he found out that he was the little girl's father.

On the other hand, finding out he used to be the type of man who treated sex as casually and offhandedly as Witt Davidson did might seriously jeopardize his new image of himself, leading to possible mental instability. Carley didn't want to be the cause of some personality disorder for the man she was learning to love all over again.

And that was the second problem she faced. Carley knew Reid would insist she rejoin the operation as soon as this latest sting was over, and that looked as though it was only a few days away. What would happen to Houston then? Reid would never allow him to simply go on as before here at the ranch.

Without his memory, Houston was too vulnerable and unprotected. Someone had thought they'd left a dead man by the side of the road eighteen months ago. What might happen if they discovered he was alive and could potentially recognize them?

Carley shivered at the thought of some unknown menace stalking an unsuspecting man. No, Reid would never allow that to happen, and the Bureau couldn't afford to permanently place a guard on a man who only thought of himself as a simple cowboy. What would become of him?

Carley decided she just couldn't bear to face the ramifications of what that might mean right now. She wanted to put the whole problem out of her mind. Shivering still, she vowed only to think of Reid's words and be Houston's protector while she could.

Carley's most immediate problem was her own attitude toward Houston. She'd made the decision to let him continue with his attempt at a new relationship on the ride back to the ranch this afternoon. That was one way for her to act as his protector for the few days they had left. It was also a way to give her a little breathing room to sort out her own emotions.

Did she really love Houston Smith as much as she thought she did? And, if she did, what had happened to her love for Witt Davidson? Could she put her old love from her mind and act as if he was gone for good? Everything about the situation was muddled in her brain. Maybe a couple of casual dates with Houston would help put her feelings into perspective.

A sharp chill shot up her spine with no warning. The secretary's words came into clear focus. Reid and the operation were nearby on the border. The shadowy figures threatening Houston might be close.

Carley stepped into her closet and dragged out her locked case. Tomorrow night Casa de Valle would be celebrating one of its teenagers' graduation from high school by having a barbecue. Houston had asked her to be his date for later that night when they chaperoned the kids at a dance in town.

She unlocked her case and pulled out her unloaded Glock, waistband holster and ammunition. If she was going to act as Houston's date—and bodyguard—she needed to be ready. Nothing would happen to the man this time. Not on her watch.

Ten

When Carley awoke from a troubled sleep, she found the morning sun refusing to shine, deferring instead to gloomy drops of rain on her windowpane. She knew Houston and the others had been praying for rain to come across the Mexican mountains and open up on the parched delta of the Rio Grande—but on the same day as the big party?

A light tickle of apprehension rode up her spine, but she refused to give it any credence. She was being silly.

As her day progressed, or in reality fell apart, that puzzling sensation she'd felt earlier turned into a downright chill. She'd hoped to see Houston at breakfast. Maybe with the rain, she'd be able to spend more of the day close to him. Protecting him. But as the staff trickled away from the table and headed toward their respective jobs, Carley grew impatient and dejected because he was nowhere to be found.

She and Gabe were the last ones at the table. Gabe eased his chair back and prepared to leave.

"Gabe, wait a second." Carley stood and moved beside him. "Do you know why Houston didn't come to breakfast this morning?"

He smiled at her. "You two getting along okay?"

"Yes, just fine. But I need to know where he is right now."

Gabe took off his glasses and stared through the lens. "The rain turned into a downpour about four in the morning, and we were worried that the hard ground wouldn't be able to take this much water all at once." He picked up a napkin and began cleaning one lens. "He and a couple of the boys went off to round up the stock. Some of the pastures have gullies and arroyos that'll flash flood without warning."

"Oh? Is he in any danger? Are we?" She wanted Gabe to quit taking his time and get to the point.

"Houston knows how to take care of himself. He'll be fine." He pushed his glasses back on his face and went to the window. "This place is high and dry. It's built to last. Besides, looks like our mixed blessing has about stopped for the day."

Carley joined him at the window and looked out as hazy sunshine filtered down through a fine mist. "Will we still have the barbecue tonight?"

Gabe turned to leave, but answered her over his shoulder. "Might be a tad muddy, but we won't let a little water stop us. You learn to be hardy when you live on the border. Some of our ancestors rode with Santa Anna and Poncho Villa. They left us with good constitutions and wills of iron. You'll get used to it in time.''

Carley knew she didn't have much time, and it made the nervous butterflies she had in her stomach all the more active. She left the kitchen and went to the phone in her office. Today was the day of her dreaded luncheon with the bureaucratic and uncooperative Ms. Fabrizio. No way could Carley keep that date, with her stomach in knots and her sense of danger increasing by the minute.

''…so I'm afraid, with the big party tonight and all the rain today, I won't be able to make our lunch.'' Carley swallowed back her tension, trying not to let it show in her voice. ''Can we make it another day?''

Ms. Fabrizio chuckled lightly into the phone. ''No problem. Maybe I'll make an exception in your case and conduct the ranch's inspection next week myself. I haven't seen the home in a couple of years. It might be very…interesting.''

What an odd character, Carley muttered as she hung up the phone. Ms. Fabrizio was just too slick, and way too hot and cold. Carley decided she'd better have Reid check into the woman's background the minute she returned to the Bureau.

Meanwhile Houston never showed up for lunch, adding to Carley's growing unease. Her sense of imminent catastrophe put everything around her in sharp and glaring focus. But she couldn't put her finger on any one thing that seemed wrong or out of place.

By midafternoon, Carley was nearly climbing out of her skin. What the heck could be so wrong, she wondered?

Doc Luisa poked her head into Carley's office. ''What're you doing stuck in here on a great day like today? The sun is shining and most of the mud is gone. Why don't you come on out and see how a real Tex-Mex barbecue is handled?''

Carley couldn't be happier to finally move. Her whole body ached from the tension of holding herself still. The two women stopped to pick up Cami from the day room. Rosie and another girl would have to miss the late-afternoon activities while they took care of their charges. Carley promised to bring them a plate of food later.

With Cami in tow, Carley and Doc headed out through the dirt yard. The ground, still hard and packed solid, held only a few puddles on the edges of the yard. Not much of a reminder of last night's downpour. The three of them slowly strolled into the 4-H barn and took their time passing by the animal pens.

"You tell Houston about Cami yet?" the older woman asked.

Carley shook her head. "There's some...complications."

Doc shook her own head in response. "Lately I've thought he was near a breakthrough in his memory. I was so hoping that you could—" She shrugged her shoulder. "Must be frustrating for all of you."

Carley didn't have time to answer as they stepped from the far side of the barn into the bright sunlight. Once her eyes adjusted, she spotted the grassy area around a pond where several of the men were busy setting things up.

And Houston Smith stood in the middle of the action. *Thank God.*

At about the same time Carley saw him, Cami pulled from Carley's grasp and took off as fast as her little legs could pump. Carley's heart began to race and she flew after her daughter. There were too many hazards out here for Cami to just run free.

Houston busied himself setting up one of the steel-drum barbecue pits. Earlier, the boys had rolled five of the unwieldy things out of the storage shed and onto the grass beyond the stock pond. As he worked, he luxuriated in the hot, dry sunshine hitting his back.

After the messy, wet morning, the day had turned clear and bright. The rainy low-pressure front pulled air with crackling, low humidity in behind it. The unusual weather wouldn't last long, he knew, but damned if it wasn't wonderful while it lasted.

The smell of wet, newly mowed grass clung in the air. The whole world seemed fresh and new—just as he wanted.

His mood reflected the current state of his life. *Carley.* Whenever he thought of her and the chance to win her love, he grew buoyantly expectant. Whatever dark shadows remained in his past could just stay buried in his unconscious. From now on he'd banish his old nightmares and find new dreams. Dreams of a good life with Carley.

Houston wondered if they would end up living on the ranch. Would Carley be able to give up her life as an FBI agent and be content to stay here, raising cattle and children? She was such an earth mother, the nurturer of all living things. Couldn't she leave the criminals of the world behind and stay in the safe cocoon of the ranch with people who loved her?

He blew out a breath and finished loading mesquite into the drum. No matter where they lived or what either of them did for a living, he knew if they were together, the sun would keep shining.

From somewhere behind him, Houston heard a high-pitched shriek. *Cami.* The other lady love of his new life. He'd know that scream anywhere.

He turned just in time to catch a glimpse of the tiny, blond head bobbing in his direction.

"Eieeee…Da…Da…"

Houston bent, scooping up the little devil, while she beamed at him. "Hey, little girl. Were you coming to see me?" He held her against his chest and breathed in the sweet smell that was all baby.

Cami held her arms straight up and bounced in his embrace. "Me…up."

"Up?" Houston studied the sweaty sweetheart in toddler-size jeans and flannel shirt. "You are up."

"More!" Cami bounced so hard he had to tighten his grip.

He turned to search for Carley. It didn't take him long to find her, striding toward them across the weedy patch of grass. She arrived breathing hard, her face flush with heat and her hair in a massive, rusty cloud swirling around that gorgeous face. "Thanks for catching Cami. I just passed my annual physical, but I guess I'm not in good enough shape to catch a one-year-old who sees something she wants."

Houston laughed. These two females were suddenly the lifeblood of his bright, new world. "I believe she started out wanting me, but now she's asking for something I don't understand." He held Cami away from his chest.

"Up!" she squealed again, and gave him her best impression of her mother's coquettish smile.

"See?" Houston turned to Carley. "What does that mean?"

It was Carley's turn to laugh. "Why, that rascal." She rested her hands on her hips and shook her head. "My grandfather throws Cami in the air every time he picks her up, even though he's past eighty and should know better. She loves it, giggles and shrieks till the rest of us want to cover our ears."

Carley held out her arms, trying to entice her daughter to leave Houston's embrace. "No, Cami. This isn't Paw-Paw. No flying today."

"Flying? Oh, I get it. Like this?" Houston adjusted his grip under her arms and lifted Cami higher. She giggled and her eyes widened. To gain a little momentum, he swung her downward in a swift movement and then threw her up over his head.

He was afraid to let her very far out of his grasp, so he kept his hands where he could reach her in an instant. Cami started to scream, and if he hadn't been able to see the look of unadulterated ecstasy on her face, Houston would've thought she was in pain. Cami's laughter was contagious, and Houston found himself laughing along with her.

After a half dozen throws of the ecstatic baby, Carley had her hands over her ears, shielding them from the high-pitched shrieks. But she grinned, and there was a deep, loving look in her eyes as she watched her baby's play. He only hoped she could spare some of that love for him.

A few minutes later Houston figured he'd better stop before the little girl got sick to her stomach. He pulled Cami to his chest, and she threw her arms around his neck and hugged him tight. It was the best feeling in the world. He bent his head, placing a kiss in the middle of all that straw-colored hair.

When Houston looked at Carley, he found silent tears welling up in her eyes. But she didn't look particularly sad.

He shifted Cami to one arm and ran a knuckle over Carley's smooth cheek. He wanted to gather mother and baby into his embrace, keeping both of them safe and warm, but he didn't imagine Carley would care much for his protective demonstrations. He'd been the one to suggest they go back to the beginning, after all.

Long fingers of lavender and rose competed with the silvery shadows of twilight in the clear sky over the Rio Grande delta. Carley sat back in her lawn chair and smiled to herself. What a wonderful afternoon it had been.

Shortly after she and Cami had arrived at the stock tank, Lloyd had appeared, leading a procession of children and teens bearing heavy bowls, pots and pans filled with all the ingredients for a real Tex-Mex barbecue. Then Lloyd had taken charge. He'd supervised the lighting of the fires, set the children to work arranging things, and all around bossed his way through the long afternoon of cooking.

Lloyd took Carley under his wing and gave her lessons in the ''proper'' way to marinate fajitas. In beer. When Carley expressed surprise at his use of alcohol on the church's ranch, he grinned at her.

''Don't nobody drink alcohol on this ranch lessen I give it to them,'' he huffed. ''Cooking takes the bite out of the brew—tenderizes the meat and adds flavor.'' He narrowed his eyebrows in mock anger. ''I keep the beer and some cooking wine under lock and key.''

Throughout the idyllic afternoon, Carley ate and laughed more than she had in years. She was really looking forward to spending some time alone with Houston later that night. All day he'd taken care to see to her every whim. When he wasn't directly catering to her and Cami's needs, he kept a watchful eye on them while attending to his other duties.

Some time ago Cami had conked out, lying down under the shade of one of the long portable tables and falling sound asleep. Carley sent her back to the main house with one of the girls, issuing a request to have Rosie put her to bed.

It had been such a lovely day, she'd almost forgotten about the foreboding chill of the stormy morning. Now, as dusk settled over the peaceful, country scene, Carley and Doc Luisa sat in lawn chairs watching the children's softball game. It took nearly all the counselors to be the coaches, and Gabe was homeplate referee. The barbecue drums were extinguished, and Lloyd and a couple of the ranch hands were cleaning and putting away the equipment.

Carley looked around and realized that for the first time she'd lost track of Houston's whereabouts. ''Have you seen Houston lately, Doc?''

The older woman nodded and pointed in the direction of a few trees on the other side of the pond. ''There he is. He's the one leaning his boot on that tree stump.''

''I see him now. Who's that he's talking to so seriously?''

''Carlos. He's the young man who graduated this week.''

Doc shifted in her chair to get a better view of the two with their heads together. "Houston's been trying to convince him to stay on at the ranch as a part-time hand while he goes to school. Bright kid. He won a full scholarship to the local, four-year college."

Carley tried to keep the surprise out of her voice, but it snuck in, anyway. "Houston's been counseling him?"

Doc gave her an unreadable look. "He's very good with the kids—patient, understanding. And he listens to their problems without being judgmental. While he teaches them about ranch work, he helps them learn to become adults."

"I see. And this young man, Carlos, he doesn't want to go to school?"

The gray-haired doctor shook her head. "It's not the school so much as the place. Carlos thinks he wants to shed himself of the country and try big-city life. He's got friends who're going to the Galveston area intent on becoming oil-rig roustabouts and making their fortunes." Doc smiled. "Houston believes Carlos is too smart to buy into that pipe dream, if only he can face reality before it's too late. My money's on Houston's persuasive talent."

"Hmm. That's a side of the man I hadn't known existed." Carley was thoughtful for a minute. She was about to ask Doc a few more questions concerning this new version of the man she loved when she noticed Rosie come barreling across the field from the barn.

Carley shut her mouth and jerked herself from the chair to start in Rosie's direction. "Rosie, what's the matter? Is it Cami? Is something wrong with her?"

By the time Rosie crossed the wide expanse to

meet them, she was out of breath and gasping for air. But she kept shaking her head while she tried to speak. "Nothing's wrong with Cami," she finally managed. "There isn't anything the matter with any of the kids, but I have to get right back. I can't leave Rachel alone with them too long."

"Then tell us why you needed to come way out here."

Carley swung around at the sound of Houston's deep voice behind her. He'd apparently seen Rosie coming, and his massive strides brought him within a few yards of them much faster than the young girl could run.

"Give her a chance," Carley cautioned him. She turned back to Rosie, who gulped for air. "Take your time. If the kids are all right and the house isn't on fire, whatever it is will wait a few seconds more."

"Some lady from the state is at the house," Rosie blurted. "I think she said her name was Ms. Fabrizio, or something." Rosie's words were choppy, but she was beginning to calm down. "She said not to bother any of you at the party, but..."

"Ms. Fabrizio? Out here at this hour on a Friday evening?" Carley didn't like the sound of this. "Did she say what brought her here?"

Rosie nodded. "She's bringing a new infant from state custody. I haven't seen the little boy yet, but she was unloading him from her van." Rosie began to wring her hands with absent and distraught movements. "I didn't think it was right for the home to get a new charge without...one of the grown-ups there. So I snuck out the kitchen door. I did right coming for you, didn't I, Miz Mills?"

"You did fine, dear." Carley laid a hand on her

shoulder. "I want you to go back now so Rachel won't be by herself. But return the same way you came out, and you and Rachel do your best to stay out of Ms. Fabrizio's sight. I'll be right along to talk to her."

Rosie looked a little panicked, so Carley added, "Don't worry. I won't tell her you came for us. Where was she when you last saw her?"

"She'd parked her van by the side door, the door by the staff parking lot. It's the closest to the infants' rooms." Rosie turned her eyes toward the house even though it was too far away to be seen. "Should I tell Preacher Diaz?"

Carley sensed Rosie's mixed feelings about going back. But she was strong. Carley knew she'd do whatever was necessary.

"I'll tell him later." Carley glanced over her shoulder to see Gabe in the middle of a heated debate at home plate. No sense bothering him now. She turned back to Rosie. "I can handle this alone. Now you scoot back to the house and quit worrying about it."

"Yes, ma'am." Rosie took off at a dead run.

"You will not." Houston's voice was close behind her—and deadly quiet.

Carley spun to face him. "What?"

"You won't be handling this alone." He laid a hand on her arm. "I'll be there with you."

She was too tense to smile, but she gently covered his hand with hers. "No reason both of us have to spoil a good evening. You stay with the kids. I'll catch up to you later."

"No, ma'am." His eyes, half-hidden in the lengthening shadows, were alive with messages she was too nervous to read. "I don't exactly know what's going on, but I can tell you're upset over it. I'm not letting you out of my sight until I know everything's okay.''

Carley opened her mouth to tell him she'd be fine, but ended up closing it before the words were uttered. The truth was, she wanted him to be beside her. Oh, Carley didn't think that Ms. Fabrizio would cause any trouble, or that she herself couldn't handle anything the lady dished out. But she'd feel better facing the unknown if Houston went along.

''All right. We'll walk over together.'' Carley turned to Doc Luisa. ''Can you stay and let Gabe know what's happened after the game's finished, Doc?''

''Sure. But would you rather I come now to check over the new infant for you?''

Carley smiled, as the kindly eyes of the dedicated doctor displayed her concern. ''No. There'll be plenty of time for that later.''

Carley's own sense of danger was intensifying by the minute. ''You could do me a favor, though. Make sure none of the children come back to the main house for a while. We'll let you know when things are all clear.''

The doctor agreed, and Houston and Carley quickly headed through the 4-H barn. The side door to the barn opened up on the far edge of the staff parking lot. Houston pulled open the heavy wooden door, and Carley was temporarily blinded by the overhead parking lot lights. When her vision cleared, she saw a commercial-type van, bathed in shadows and parked next to the side door of the main house.

Though the night was warm and turning sultry, Carley felt a sudden chill wind. None of this seemed right. Her hand automatically went to her waistband holster. She let her fingers tighten around the smooth, metal gun handle, but left the weapon strapped in place. Maybe she was being silly and there was a perfectly reasonable explanation for all of this.

Carley and Houston took a few tentative steps toward the van. They were still cloaked in the barn's shadow, and they found themselves silently stealing forward an inch at a time. Carley felt as if she could wrap herself in the suspense that hung in the air.

Before they reached the edge of their cover of darkness, a woman stepped from the side door of the house and headed around the front of the van. The light was particularly bright by the door, and Carley and Houston both caught a clear view of her.

The woman was about Carley's height and build, but instead of auburn hair, hers was black and cropped short in the back. She glanced around quickly as if she was nervous. Her eyes were every bit as black as her hair. They were flat and cold, not lifeless, but—mean.

Carley heard a soft gasp from the man walking next to her. Houston reached out and stopped her from moving any further into the light.

"Something's very wrong here. I know that woman," he whispered.

Eleven

Carley stood perfectly still, but turned her face to whisper back at Houston. "'Know her' from where? How?"

"I don't know how or where. But she's the woman in my dreams…my nightmares."

Carley's instincts went on full alert. She couldn't let Houston get mixed up in whatever lay ahead. "Go back through the barn and get to a phone. Call the local field office of the FBI. Ask to be patched through to Reid Sorrels. Tell him Agent Mills said it's an emergency and she needs assistance."

"No." He stepped closer to her and tightly gripped her elbow. "I said I'm not leaving you."

She couldn't see the look in his eyes because of the shadows over his face, but she could hear the tone in his voice, telling her all the things he didn't have time to say. Carley turned her head to survey the area, hesitating to issue a direct order to the man she loved, but at the same time needing to keep him safe.

The fact that Ms. Fabrizio had brought a baby to the ranch without notifying anyone made Carley more than a little suspicious. But that she'd deliberately timed it to be in the middle of a Friday night party made Carley's thoughts turn to baby-stealers and rumors about the ranch. Houston's wariness of the woman clinched it for her.

Carley laid a hand on her hidden weapon again, but she didn't want any trouble here on the ranch with the children and Houston in harm's way. Ms. Fabrizio appeared to be alone. Carley wondered if Reid was close by. She had a gut feeling this woman was the one he'd been seeking.

"Who's out there?" Ms. Fabrizio shouted in their direction. Too late to do anything else, Carley decided to try talking her way out of the problem.

"It's only me, Carley Mills, Ms. Fabrizio." Carley stepped forward and, in a few feet, left the shadows for the brightly lit parking lot. Houston was so close to her she could feel the tension coming from his body. "I'm surprised to see you. I thought you weren't coming out here till next week," she said, then managed a fake smile.

Ms Fabrizio peered at them as they neared the van. In a second she straightened, pointing her finger at Houston.

"You?"

Houston stopped dead. The sound of her voice reverberated in his ears. A door to his mind cracked open, letting out shards of broken memories. Each one whizzed around his brain, a kaleidoscope of hazy red faces and blurry blue memories. Everything was moving too fast. He couldn't speak.

Ms. Fabrizio didn't have any such trouble with her voice. "Alberto! Get out here! Come see a walking ghost."

She'd turned to call out, and as she turned back, her hand withdrew a gun from her jacket pocket. And she pointed it directly at Houston's head.

Houston could feel Carley freeze beside him, but he couldn't focus on any of his current surroundings. Vivid images assailed his mind, bombarding him with information from every side.

A hulking, dark man stepped out of the shadowy light on the far side of the van. When he spotted Houston, his lips curled up into a wide, yellow-toothed grin. "Ah. *Mi amigo muerto.*"

"We left you dead once, lawman. Looks like we muffed the job." Ms. Fabrizio motioned to her ugly, overweight henchman. "Knock him out and throw him in the back of the van. We don't have anything to tie him with, so make sure he's out cold. And don't make another mistake. Once is enough for any man to beat death."

She turned to Carley. "I'm afraid you stepped into the middle of something that isn't any of your business, sweetie. Now we won't have any choice but to have you meet with the same accident as your boyfriend here. Too bad. I kinda hoped you and I could come to some arrangement. It would have been very profitable…for both of us."

The next moment everything exploded around Houston in a blur of activity. The heavyset man swung a solid object at Houston's head, landing a blow across his ear and buckling his legs under him.

As he dropped to his knees, Houston saw Carley ram the giant with a quick upper cut to his chin. Alberto staggered backward against Ms. Fabrizio's weapon, discharging it directly into his own back.

"Move. Move. Move." Carley's voice burst from her lips as she commanded him to get up. Houston's legs felt disembodied, black nothingness obscured his vision. He struggled to his feet as Carley half dragged him around the corner of the house, pulling her weapon from its holster as she went.

Using the house itself as a shield, Carley pulled them both down to the ground. Houston leaned against the Mexican bricks of the house and fought to form a coherent thought.

Carley squatted beside him and gently touched her fingers to his head. "You're bleeding. I knew I should never have let you come with me."

"Carley." His voice was shaky, rough in his own ears. He cleared his throat.

"Can you get up?" She peeked around the corner, back to where they'd just come from. "Looks like the giant is down for the count. Our gun-toting bureaucrat is dragging him into the cover behind the van."

"Why didn't you take her into custody when she fell off balance...instead of taking cover yourself?" His voice was stronger now.

Carley glanced back at him, then quickly returned her gaze to the van and the woman it sheltered. "I couldn't take a chance on her shooting you while you were down. Do you think you can make it to the back door? I need you to lock the doors from the inside and then call Reid. Can you do it?"

He put his hand on Carley's shoulder and squeezed.

"Give me the gun and go make the call. You can get through to him faster than I can."

She shook off his hand, but didn't turn around. "No. No. It'll be fine. Just get the operator to patch you directly to the field office."

He almost smiled at her bravado. Carley was definitely a goddess.

"Hand over your weapon, Special Agent Charleston Mills." He put all the authority into the words that he could muster, considering the pain in the side of his head.

She spun around, her eyes wide with shock. "Witt?"

He did smile then, but he wasn't sure she could see in the ever-darkening twilight. "I remember." He put a hand on her arm to reassure her. "It's coming back in waves, but I've recaptured nearly everything."

"Oh, my God. Witt!"

He slid the Glock from her grip. "Now get in the house and lock the doors. I've always been a better shot than you and, besides, I've got a little score to settle with Ms. Fabrizio."

Carley's mouth opened and shut a couple of times before she quickly changed places with him. "I need to check on the kids," she squeaked.

Turning to steal away, she stopped, jerking her head back to him for one last parting remark. "But only in your wildest dreams are you a better shot than I am, buster. And don't you forget it."

Witt chuckled at her words as he watched her scurry to the kitchen door. When she disappeared into the relative safety of the house, he turned back to his immediate problem.

Ms. Fabrizio had hunkered down, leaving the van

between them. With the rapidly approaching veil of darkness, she could easily get into the van and maybe get away before he could stop her. Or worse, she might get inside the house's side door before Carley could lock it. He needed a little time—and a little luck.

"FBI. Drop your weapon and come out, Fabrizio. Keep your hands where I can see them." Witt doubted that she would comply with his commands, but it was as good a start as any.

"You've got to be kidding. I had you punished the last time for hiding in my truck. This time you deserve torture for making me hurt Alberto. I'm not going anywhere without you, Mr. FBI."

A picture of her standing, with a gun pointed directly at his head, while Alberto and another man beat him to a bloody pulp blotted out the glare of the halogen lights that were throwing eerie shadows on the parking lot. Witt shook his head. The resulting sharp pain brought him back to his current situation.

He needed to get Ms. Fabrizio out in the open— and away from the house and the children. He was about to tell her he'd give up so she would take him captive and drive them both away from here, when all hell broke loose. Three plain sedans roared into the parking lot, effectively cutting off Ms. Fabrizio's avenue of escape. From his vantage point, Witt could see Reid Sorrels and a couple of other fellows he recognized leaving the cars with their weapons drawn.

Ms. Fabrizio spun with her weapon pointed at the newcomers, but when she saw how outgunned and unprotected she really was, she threw the gun down and raised her arms above her head. At that instant Carley opened the house's side door, steadily holding her backup weapon pointed directly at the woman's head.

"Hold perfectly still, Ms. Fabrizio," Carley demanded somberly. "So far you've been lucky this is a children's home. No one wants to discharge a weapon here. But I'd just love to pay you back for all the pain you've caused, so please don't move."

Carley took a deep breath and let it out with a sigh. The past twenty-four hours had been a blur of activity with precious little rest. The answers to all the questions from Reid, from Gabe and from all the others at the ranch left her throat sore and her head hurting.

Upstairs in her bedroom Carley fought the urge to flop down on the bed in hysterics. She and Cami had to pack. They'd be leaving the ranch tomorrow.

Worse yet, she hadn't had a chance to talk to Houston. No…she had to keep reminding herself he wasn't Houston anymore. There would never be another chance to talk to Houston Smith. Witt Davidson had been the one spirited away to a local psychiatric hospital for observation and tests.

Carley wasn't concerned about Witt's health. She knew how tough he was. Instead she worried herself sick about what on earth to say to him, now that Witt had returned to his old personality.

More than worried—miserable and inconsolable came closer to describing what she was feeling. She and Houston had been so close to a relationship worth giving up everything for. Now she'd never get the chance to tell him she loved him. That man was gone for good.

Carley sighed deep within her chest and tried to hold back a sob. *Dear God. He is truly gone.* Never again would Houston's arms enfold her in their safe embrace. Never again would she know the pleasure of being treated like a rare gem.

She swiped a hand across the wetness streaking her cheeks. The image of him gazing warily down at her the first time they'd met appeared behind her closed eyes and made her want to groan.

She shook her head to clear it, but flashes of the two of them together came unbidden. Mental pictures of him at the roadhouse, of him holding Cami on the mare and of him bracing himself above her as he stroked her bare skin left her breathless and blurry-eyed.

She sniffed and straightened her shoulders. This was exactly what she couldn't have happen. How could she explain any of it to Witt?

"Mama?" Cami toddled over and patted her calf. "All better?"

Carley wrapped her daughter in a tight hug. "It'll be okay, Cami. Mama will get through this...for you."

Shaking her head, Carley opened a dresser drawer and pulled out one of Cami's favorite dolls. "Here, baby. Play with Samantha while Mommy starts packing our bags." Carley sniffed back the tears as she handed Cami the doll and some doll clothes. She hoped Cami would be content on the floor so she could get a head start on tomorrow.

As she wrestled her wheeled duffel from the closet, she vowed to tell the man about Cami the instant he showed up. Now that he was back to being the old Witt, he probably wouldn't want the responsibility of a child, anyway. Besides that, she could never make a life with a man she didn't love.

She thought back to when she first arrived at the ranch, remembering how she'd been so sure she loved Witt, so positive she could make him remember and love her, too. A sob, masquerading as a chuckle, escaped her lips. She hadn't even known what true love—the heart aching and forevermore kind—was all about until she'd learned to know Houston.

Carley did know Witt to be an honorable man, though, one who'd make arrangements to visit his daughter and support her to adulthood.

She swiped at her eyes as tears began to spill again. Damn, but she would miss Houston. He'd gotten under her skin, seeping into her soul and ruining her for any other lover. Never again could she settle for the casual treatment of a man like Witt Davidson.

No matter what, there was no going back to the way it had been before Witt disappeared from her life. She and Cami would live their lives alone. Thank heaven for Cami. Her daughter was now her sole reason to stay alive and go on.

She unzipped the suitcase, laid it on the bed and began haphazardly pitching underwear inside. Reid had insisted she be back at work in Houston on Monday. Two state Child Protective Services people and a new psychologist were coming to the ranch to dig through the mess in the foster home files.

The Bureau was, right this minute, searching for Dan Lattimer, the ranch's former psychologist. They had lots of questions to pose to the man. Due to the lax record-keeping, Ms. Fabrizio had been running illegal children in and out of the home like a way station on their route to clandestine adoptions. She'd been a major player in the international child-abduction ring.

"Uh…may I come in?" Witt moved through the doorway without waiting for an answer.

When he saw the suitcase open on the bed, he closed the door quietly behind him. "You going somewhere?" He couldn't let her leave yet. There was too much to say. Too much at stake.

"Cami and I are leaving for Houston the day after tomorrow. Are you going back right away, too, or are you taking some time off?" Carley continued folding clothes into her suitcase.

Witt hesitated. Apparently she'd only come to the ranch to find him because of her job. He'd lost his chance with her a long time ago.

Still…he had to say what was on his mind.

"Carley, can you stop and listen to me a second?"

She whirled around. "First, I have something to say."

"Can't it wait a few minutes? I have to get this off my chest now." He deliberately softened his voice. Demanding was no way to tell her. "Please."

Her shoulders relaxed and she looked up at him with those blinding green eyes. It took every ounce of his strength to keep from dragging her to his chest.

"I need for you to hear the real story about that last night when I disappeared from the mission." Suddenly he was too nervous to look her in the eyes. He didn't normally talk about what was on his mind.

"After I found Fabrizio's truck hidden in the woods, I decided to sneak into the truck's bed rather than just call for backup." He glanced down at his hands and found them shaking, so he jammed them in his jeans pockets. "I tried telling myself that my unorthodox actions were because Fabrizio had heard all the commotion and was getting ready to bolt."

He chuckled at his own foolishness. "I really knew better. I did it because it was a good excuse to get away from you for a little while."

Carley gasped lightly and closed her eyes. His hands came out of his pockets and instinctively reached for her. He managed to stop himself just in time.

"I…" He cleared his throat and started again. "I don't mean to hurt you any more than I already have, but I need to tell you the truth. All of it.

"You scared the heck out of me that last night, Carley. All that talk about marriage and the look in your eyes… Well, it got to me. My heart ached for you, but love had always caused me nothing but pain in the past. I couldn't take a chance on it again."

She looked up at him with tears in her eyes. He was hurting her again, but there wasn't anything he could do to stop it. He had to get it all said—had to do right, for once in his life.

"Fabrizio and her buddy drove straight back to the Rio Grande Valley. Six hours I lay flattened in the back of that truck waiting for a chance to sneak out and call for backup." Witt couldn't stand to face her. He tried looking over her shoulder. "By the time they stopped for gas, it was nearly broad daylight. They spotted me and had me knocked out and back in the truck before I could get away.

"I don't remember anything else until I woke two weeks later in Doc Luisa's bed. The doctors think I may never get the actual shooting back."

"Witt…"

"No. Let me finish." His voice lowered to a raspy whisper. "When I woke up with no memories…no background or mental baggage…I made a conscious decision to become the best man I could be. With Doc Luisa's help I turned myself into a brand-new person. I picked all the attributes my subconscious mind must have admired all along. I became a good man, one who could accept and give love.''

"Witt, you were always a good man. Please, I must tell you something right now.'' Carley broke into his thoughts.

He waved her off. "Just one more minute.'' He swallowed hard and got ready to really open himself up for the pain he knew was coming. He deserved it. "Now that I remember everything, I don't want to go back to being that man who ran out on you. I can't. I can never go back to being the Witt you fell in love with…not even if it means I have to live without you.''

At his last words Witt thought he saw a look in her eyes that confirmed what he'd feared. She'd loved the old Witt Davidson, and now that he was gone her love had died.

But he couldn't stand so close to his dream and not try. "Don't leave me, my love. Give us a chance. Stay and get to know the new Witt. You might learn to love him as much as the old one.''

Before he could stop himself, he'd pulled her to him and held her close. He rubbed his cheek against hers and stopped breathing. "Please tell me I don't have to live without you.''

Carley was weak in the knees and nearly speechless. *Thank the Lord*. The man she loved hadn't disappeared. Just because he had Witt Davidson's name and memories didn't mean he couldn't be the man she'd come to love.

Her whole body sagged as relief washed over her,

and Carley was in heaven. Almost. There was still one more thing. And it might just change his mind about her.

"I…" She pulled back from his embrace and took a minute to find her voice. "Before I answer you, there's still something I must tell you."

"All right. I know you want to tell me about Cami's father. I can bear to hear it now because I've accepted that it was my fault you were left alone and lonely. I'm strong enough to take the worst." He glanced away for just a second. "I don't blame you for finding solace in someone else's arms. It must have been horrible for you when I just disappeared like that."

Before she could speak, a crashing noise disturbed the quiet. They both jerked toward the sound.

"Cami!"

Witt beat Carley to the closet. "What are you up to, little one?" He reached in and scooped Cami up in his arms. When they reentered the bedroom, Cami had a picture frame clutched in her fingers. "Are you okay, Cami?"

The toddler looked up at him with those big gray-green eyes and then looked at the photograph in her hand. She laid her other palm flat down on the glass. "Daddy."

Witt took the photograph from her with his free hand. He studied it a minute. "Carley, this is a picture of me taken at one of Reid's pool parties in Houston. You kept it with you all this time?"

Carley didn't get the chance to answer. She could see Witt making the connections in his mind. He looked at the picture of himself, then examined Cami.

Back and forth, he scrutinized every feature of both faces.

"Cami...Camille. *My* mother's name was Camille."

He turned a stricken look to Carley, and her knees started to shake. "She's my child, isn't she? There never was another man."

Oh, no. Carley couldn't lose him now that they were so close to the happiness she knew they could have. "Witt, let me explain. I tried to tell—"

"I'm a dad! I'm really Cami's daddy. I didn't force you into someone else's arms. Thank God." Witt swung Cami around the room, laughing and dancing.

Cami shrieked. Witt wiped tears from his cheeks with the back of his hand. And Carley finally relaxed.

It turned out she *was* crazy. Crazy in love with the man who lit up her life. The man who meant everything.

Witt stopped twirling as suddenly as he'd begun. He stepped to her side, tentatively searching her eyes. "Do you think you can learn to love the new me as much as you did the man who fathered your child?"

Carley nodded. "More. I'll never love another man as much as I love you. I'm so full of love for you right now I'm afraid I might burst."

Relief flooded his eyes. "Then take pity on the man who needs you more than breathing. You and Cami and I are getting married...tomorrow."

"Tomorrow? But how...where?"

"Las Vegas. Just finish packing your bags and leave everything else to me. We're going to bind ourselves together...in the eyes of the law. I'll go call your grandparents and start making arrangements."

He handed over Cami and then dragged his lips

across hers in a blazing kiss. "Keep that in mind while I'm gone. I'll be back soon."

And Carley knew that this time "soon" was about to turn into a forever commitment, bringing with it a lifetime full of passion, love and joy.

Epilogue

Four Years Later

"**M**om! Daddy's coming up the road...and Auntie Doc's with him."

Carley wiped her hands off and untied her apron. "Good spotting, Cam. Now run upstairs and tell the rest of the kids it's time to be going. I just want to change the twins, then they'll be ready, too."

Cami's boots squealed as she spun on the kitchen tile.

"And put on your dress shoes."

"Aw, Mom."

"Don't 'Aw, Mom' me, young lady. Do it. And don't rip that new dress." Carley chuckled when she was positive her daughter could no longer hear her.

In spite of Carley's best efforts, Cami had become

a real tomboy. Actually, *cowgirl* would be a better description. Cami's devotion to her father had shown up in her attempts to emulate him. Instead of party dresses and dolls, her fondest ambition right now was to become a barrel racer in the state rodeo.

Sighing, Carley put her apron aside and picked up one of her beautiful, eighteen-month-old boys. Their carrot-orange, curly hair and wide green eyes made her smile every time she looked at them. Houston and Chess were going to be the spitting images of the father she never knew. Carley wondered whether they'd also love all things Western like their sister, or if maybe their high-tech genes would win out.

The screen door sprung open, and Carley looked up at the man who filled her kitchen the same way he'd filled her life and her heart. "Where's Doc?" she asked.

"She stopped to check on Cami's new kittens. She'll be right along."

Witt stepped to her and pressed his body against her backside as she leaned over one of the babies. "Don't I get a welcome home kiss, wife?"

Keeping one hand firmly on the squirmy toddler, she turned into her husband's wide embrace. Witt covered her mouth with his, deepened the kiss and blasted coherent thought from her mind. What had she ever done to get this lucky?

When Witt finally raised his head, Carley gazed at the passionately lustful look in his eyes. "You've only been gone an hour. What's all this about?"

He shrugged one shoulder. "Can't I give my wife a quick, hot kiss before we're inundated with kids?" Witt scrutinized her while he reached for the other twin.

"Besides, you're looking particularly ravishing today. You doing something different with your hair?"

Carley smiled inwardly. Her secret would have to wait until tonight. There wouldn't be time to tell Witt before Carlos's college graduation ceremony.

"Daddy!" Chess had inched off the counter and stood pulling on Witt's pants leg as the man tried to change a screaming Houston.

Carley quickly finished the tabs on the diaper Witt had been fumbling with, just as thundering hordes of children stomped down the stairs and into the kitchen. Voices were raised, dogs barked, kids quarreled.

Witt loved every minute of it. He loved raising his own kids alongside their precious foster children. Every day was filled with some new wonder when one of the kids discovered love and caring for the first time. Witt couldn't imagine living any other way.

He glanced around at the young faces, loving the differences he found there—brown eyes and skin on one skinny little girl; deep-set, coal-colored eyes on one chubby boy; and ruddy, square jaws on the serious faces of the other two boys. The Davidsons' own little Rainbow Coalition. Every one of them so earnest and serious. Life was good for all of them here in the big house he'd built with his own hands on a far corner of the church property.

Then Witt glanced up to see his darling Carley, standing in the midst of the confusion and soaking up the children's youthful exuberance. What a woman she was. Mother, counselor, mediator…lover. He was suddenly overcome with the most fervent tenderness toward her he'd ever felt.

"What's all this commotion?" Doc Luisa bustled into the kitchen. She took one look at Carley and shoved her fists on her hips. "Well I'll be, why didn't someone tell me you were expecting again, girl? I'll need to plan my practice around getting another patient from you in a few months."

Witt's mouth dropped open. He swung around to look at his wife. Carley's face blushed pink, and she only smiled at him, so he took a better look. Yep. There was that telltale roundness to her body and that special, Madonna quality to Carley that she'd had for both her other pregnancies.

He chuckled lightly at the thought of how he'd reacted the first time he'd seen that quality, nearly six years ago in a cheap motel on the outskirts of Houston. He remembered the pure, unadulterated panic he'd felt at the time. Now...now his body reacted with heat and his heart reacted with sweet achings.

Why hadn't he noticed before?

He moved to his wife's side and slipped an arm around her waist. "When were you planning on informing the Daddy?" he whispered.

Carley raised those sexy, pine-green eyes to his. "Tonight, Daddy. When I could get you alone."

The thrill that jolted through him every time she came this close nearly knocked him over. "Couldn't we..." He had to clear his throat. "How about coming upstairs with me right now. Doc can take the kids to the graduation."

Carley shook her head and bestowed one of her dreamy smiles on him. "Later. Carlos would be devastated if we didn't show up for his graduation. You're the reason he finished and decided to go on to veterinary school."

Witt leaned his forehead against hers and let the deep emotions wash between them. If he lived for a thousand years, he'd never tire of loving this woman and needing to keep her close. She was his life, his every reason for being alive.

With a laugh and a quick kiss, Carley began to bustle her whole brood out the door.

And as he helped her shoo kids into the van, Witt Davidson thanked the Lord for the real happiness that comes when loving a woman makes you a better man.

*   *   *   *   *

*Watch for Linda Conrad's next
sexy Silhouette Desire,
DESPERADO DAD,
out in August 2002!*

Silhouette Desire

presents

DYNASTIES: THE CONNELLYS

A brand-new miniseries about the Connellys of Chicago, a wealthy, powerful American family tied by blood to the royal family of the island kingdom of Altaria. They're wealthy, powerful and rocked by scandal, betrayal…and passion!

Look for a whole year of glamorous and utterly romantic tales in 2002:

Silhouette
Where love comes alive™

Visit Silhouette at www.eHarlequin.com

SDDYN02

Silhouette® Desire

Continues the captivating series from
bestselling author
BARBARA McCAULEY

SECRETS!

Hidden legacies, hidden loves—revel in the
unfolding of the Blackhawk siblings' deepest, most
desirable SECRETS!

Don't miss the next irresistible books in the series...

TAMING BLACKHAWK
On Sale May 2002
(SD #1437)

IN BLACKHAWK'S BED
On Sale July 2002
(SD #1447)

And look for another title on sale in 2003!

Available at your favorite retail outlet.

Silhouette®
Where love comes alive™

SDSEC02

If you enjoyed what you just read,
then we've got an offer you can't resist!

Take 2 bestselling love stories FREE!

Plus get a FREE surprise gift!

Clip this page and mail it to Silhouette Reader Service™

IN U.S.A.
3010 Walden Ave.
P.O. Box 1867
Buffalo, N.Y. 14240-1867

IN CANADA
P.O. Box 609
Fort Erie, Ontario
L2A 5X3

YES! Please send me 2 free Silhouette Desire® novels and my free surprise gift. After receiving them, if I don't wish to receive anymore, I can return the shipping statement marked cancel. If I don't cancel, I will receive 6 brand-new novels every month, before they're available in stores! In the U.S.A., bill me at the bargain price of $3.34 plus 25¢ shipping and handling per book and applicable sales tax, if any*. In Canada, bill me at the bargain price of $3.74 plus 25¢ shipping and handling per book and applicable taxes**. That's the complete price and a savings of at least 10% off the cover prices—what a great deal! I understand that accepting the 2 free books and gift places me under no obligation ever to buy any books. I can always return a shipment and cancel at any time. Even if I never buy another book from Silhouette, the 2 free books and gift are mine to keep forever.

225 SEN DFNS
326 SEN DFNT

Name	(PLEASE PRINT)	
Address	Apt.#	
City	State/Prov.	Zip/Postal Code

* Terms and prices subject to change without notice. Sales tax applicable in N.Y.
** Canadian residents will be charged applicable provincial taxes and GST.
  All orders subject to approval. Offer limited to one per household and not valid to current Silhouette Desire® subscribers.
  ® are registered trademarks of Harlequin Enterprises Limited.

DES01   ©1998 Harlequin Enterprises Limited

COMING NEXT MONTH

#1447 IN BLACKHAWK'S BED—Barbara McCauley
Man of the Month/Secrets!
Experience had taught loner Seth Blackhawk not to believe in happily-ever-after. Then one day he saved the life of a little girl. Hannah Michaels, the child's mother, sent desire surging through him. But did he have the courage to accept the love she offered?

**#1448 THE ROYAL & THE RUNAWAY BRIDE—
Kathryn Jensen**
Dynasties: The Connellys
Vowing not to be used for her money again, Alexandra Connelly ran away to Altaria and posed as a horse trainer. There she met sexy Prince Phillip Kinrowan, whose intoxicating kisses made her dizzy with desire. The irresistible prince captured her heart, and she longed for the right moment to tell him the truth about herself.

#1449 COWBOY'S SPECIAL WOMAN—Sara Orwig
Nothing had prepared wanderer Jake Reiner for the sizzling attraction between him and Maggie Langford. Her beauty and warmth tempted him, and soon he yearned to claim her. Somehow he had to convince her that he wanted her—not just for today, but for eternity!

#1450 THE SECRET MILLIONAIRE—Ryanne Corey
Wealthy cop Zack Daniels couldn't believe his luck when he found himself locked in a basement with leggy blonde Anna Smith. Things only got better as she offered him an undercover assignment…as her boyfriend-of-convenience. Make-believe romance soon turned to real passion, but what would happen once his temporary assignment ended?

#1451 CINDERELLA & THE PLAYBOY—Laura Wright
Abby McGrady was stunned when millionaire CEO C. K. Tanner asked her to be his pretend wife so he could secure a business deal. But after unexpected passion exploded between them, Abby found herself falling for devastatingly handsome Tanner. She wanted to make their temporary arrangement permanent. Now she just had to convince her stubborn bachelor he wanted the same thing.

#1452 ZANE: THE WILD ONE—Bronwyn Jameson
A good man was proving hard to find for Julia Goodwin. Then former bad boy Zane Lucas came back to town. Their attraction boiled over when circumstances threw them together, and they spent one long, hot night together. But Julia wanted forever, and dangerous, sexy-as-sin Zane wasn't marriage material…or was he?

SDCNM0602